Curfew and

Sean O'Reilly was born in 1969 in Derry. He currently lives in Dublin. His first novel, *Love and Sleep*, will be published by Faber in 2002.

Curfew
and Other Stories

SEAN O'REILLY

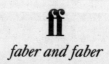

faber and faber

First published in Great Britain in 2000
by Faber and Faber Limited
3 Queen Square London WC1N 3AU
This paperback edition first published in 2001

An early draft of 'Curfew' appeared in *Stand* magazine (Spring 1998)
and 'The Good News' appeared in *The Phoenix Book of Irish Short Stories 1999*
(ed. David Marcus).

Typeset by Faber and Faber
Printed in England by Mackays of Chatham plc.

A CIP record for this book
is available from the British Library

ISBN 0–571–20654–9

2 4 6 8 10 9 7 5 3 1

I would like to express my thanks to
Gerald Dawe and Brendan Kennelly at the Oscar
Wilde Centre for Irish Writing, Dublin.

Heavenly Hurt, it gives us—
We can find no scar,
But internal difference,
Where the Meanings, are—

EMILY DICKINSON

Contents

A Charmer

This old man who said he was a Devine was the one who found Brendan early on the Sunday morning, in his best suit and shoes and the overcoat I gave him for the winter, not a hair out of place, on his knees among the seagulls up near the new bridge. The rain was lashing down on them in the rancid light, he said, when he stopped and tried to entice Brendan into a conversation, hoping to be lucky enough at long last to meet someone at the mercy of a more ostentatious sorrow than his own. He looked at me suddenly with a warning in his fat mildewed eyes and I found myself nodding in sympathy without knowing why. I talked to him in a pub on Foundling Road I never knew existed, about a fortnight after Brendan was buried. I had noticed Devine at the wake hand in hand with Father Pelonovitch but it had taken me this long to track him down. A dirty-looking tear swelled up in the corner of his eye as he told me how he had reluctantly given up on any hope of dialogue and continued his walk along the fruitless water, not wanting to interrupt a young lad in the harmless contempla- tion of his own travesty. When he returned along the same way some time later, he discovered that Brendan was still coldly disinclined to any talk and it was not less than two hours after that, he insisted with a hairy clenched fist, of marvelling at the young lad's sodden distress, that he finally understood the way things stood, or knelt in the mire, and reached into Brendan's pocket for his dole card in its handy plastic cover.

To escape briefly from the sight of the heart-shaped pool of snotter forming under his yellowing nose, I went to the bar and ordered Devine another drink. I held out my hand with the money and the barman—he looked like one of the Browns from Milk Row—grabbed hold of my wrist and informed me that 'I know all about you, woman. You fucken make one wrong move and I'll fucken smash your face in myself, woman or not.' Back at the table I was forced to watch as Devine stuck his hand in his mouth and foraged around excitedly like he was on the verge of getting hold of something interesting. Then I asked him what had happened when Brendan's family turned up. He was surprised to see so many of them he said, staring grumpily at his slimy hand, he had counted at least twenty of them, struggling through the rain and the muck in their good clothes, caught on their way out the door to early mass. I must have been smiling there for Devine stopped talking and I was forced to explain that the Mc Shanes were always a fanatical lot and liked to be first at the altar for the tastiest stuff fresh from the oven. That was a rash thing to do and I disliked myself for it; there are few worse things than talking behind people's backs.

It was the eldest sister Majella who prevented anyone ringing to let me know what had happened, her own mother admitted that to me at the wake, so I was denied my right to see Brendan at his picturesque genuflection in the weeds and slime and stones and rubbish. Devine described the scene badly, he said merely that the Mc Shanes were all very subdued and tearful in amongst the gulls who stuck to their ground and screamed and pecked and snapped at their ankles, the rain changed to sleet and then back again, one of the girls threw a glove into the idle water and the bells went for first mass. Winking at me mysteriously, he said that an argument had started between the family members about whether or not the police should be called, which culminated in one of the girls, Majella I bet, pushing one of the men over on the rocks and lashing around with her rosary beads in defence of the kneeling figure of her brother. I would have been in the kitchen with my own mother, putting on the dinner, taking out her curlers, helping my father get himself ready, wishing I was somewhere else. I would have been asleep in bed in all my clothes at the hour Brendan joined his hands and the water rubbed and rubbed against his pointed throat.

The first time we met was in Lilly the Crook's windowless shop in the shadow of the cathedral. I was standing behind him while Lilly was doing her sums on a stack of brown paper bags. I have to say I liked the way he handled her usual protests that it was unthinkable and preposterous that she might have undercharged him, the patient and sincere voice he used to persuade her to take the money in his hand and she could knock it off his bill the next time he was in. Lilly was still sceptically considering this proposal as if she was hearing it for the first time when a bottle must have flown in through the door and smashed at my feet. I screamed and covered my head. The shop darkened immediately as a saracen screeched to a stop right outside the little doorway. Bastards, I heard Lilly whisper in the darkness, as though the word was a secret password, and immediately a squall of bricks and bottles clattered against the engine and the walls outside. The three of us waited in silence and counted the rhythmical pattering bursts; after the sixth we heard the whine of another saracen approaching up the hill, there was some distant shouting and then a stillness which was when I realised I was holding on, not tightly, not in fear or panic, to a cock, half-hardened, slim, warm behind the zip of his trousers.

We walked up the hill together. He was dressed neatly, shaven, his shoes were polished; his hair was clean and combed but badly cut along the fringe. A long neck gave him height and half way up it the taut bump of his apple protruded like a second and stronger chin and forced him to hold his head back at an awkward angle as if he was a keen surveyor of the hectic sameness above the slates and chimneys and the black bones of the aerials. It made me wonder, his aloft gaze, whether he carried a bruise on his narrow chest from when he bowed his head to pray for he was obviously one of those who bent easily at the knee. His skin was white, starved, a quick nick of a mouth but there was a sense of relief when you met his eyes with the haze in them, a looming blankness he had to blink away every few minutes. Still embarrassed by my waywardness, I attempted to make a joke and accused him of being drunk because of the mist in his eyes but like a dog turning a windy corner he shook his head and sniffed and informed me that he never drank. That was probably the only interesting thing he said, if not the only thing. I was the one who was left to do all the talking. By the time we reached the brow of the hill I was tired out and hoping I'd see the back of him soon. Then, out of some vicious sense of politeness or havoc, I pointed up the road to our house and told him to drop in some day for a cup of tea if he had nothing better to do. I had to tell him my name and then ask about his. I knew one of his uncles, Patsy, who worked in the butcher's on Clear Street. I went back to the house and forgot all about him until about a month or so later when I open the door and there he is, stood well back in the road and wondering if I want to go for a walk with him out the back roads. I thought he was joking. Who goes for walks these days? Wait till I get my bucket and we'll pick some berries, I said to him, imagining myself in a starched white apron and hobnailed boots. He stayed for a couple of hours drinking tea in the kitchen and barely said a word.

6

– So are you working? I say to him knowing full well he isn't but desperate for something to talk about.

– Me? he says stiffening.

I think I might have laughed at this point for he leans forward slightly and there is a trembling harshness in his eyes which I don't mind and says firmly to me, I've never worked a day in my life.

– That's great, I say. I've lost count.

He swallows some tea and the bulge in his neck sinks and stalls and then slowly ascends again like his poor bloated body would one morning out of the sagging bobbing slapping water.

– So how old are you then? I come up with next.

There is a long pause. He looks away from me solemnly. I watch him staring at the sink or my mother's skirts on the line or the slight swaying of the golden tassel on the blind string. I pour myself more tea. I watch him some more.

– Is that a bad question? I finally have to confront him. Aren't I allowed to ask you that or what?

He looks confused suddenly, blinking rapidly, joining his hands.

– Your age? I say and try to smile.

– Thirty-two, he tells me simply and then smiles and shakes his head in wonder. I lower my eyes to give him the chance but he makes no attempt to inquire after mine.

There were a few times his big lean head twisted round towards the door. I don't know what it was that kept me from asking what he was expecting to see. It wasn't until I knew him better that it occurred to me that he was serious about the walk.

We saw each other practically every day after that, calmly, carefully, without exuberance or haste or guile. I was working as a receptionist in Quigleys' around this time. Neither of us was fond of sitting in the same pub every night so we usually ended up walking the streets or occupying the front room of my house, because his was too crowded he always claimed. In that cold and sullen room by the light of the electric fire, Brendan seemed content to admire the blighted choreography of our breaths in front of the window. Now and again, footsteps or voices briefly filled the room with dreary mysteries when people passed outside. I had never been with a man who seemed to want so little of me. Some women might be grateful for that but I was tormented by the feeling that he was waiting on something, that his interest in me amounted to no more than a confused desire for my security or my safety, like a strange man who waits silently with you for the taxi to take you home. One night, to cheer us up, I brought in a radio and sat down beside him and took his long frozen hand and placed it around my waist. After about half an hour nothing had happened.

– Brendan, what do you want?

Frowning, he looks down at me with my head on his shoulder and then away again at the radio, like a small limbless creature on the floor in front of us. I think I'm giving him time to consider his response. The man on the radio is reading out the names of ones arrested.

– Brendan?

– Aye I know, he says sadly, swallowing. Seamy Gallagher wouldn't hurt a fly.

– I don't give a damn about Seamy Gallagher; maybe he would have done bloody better anyway to hurt a fly or two.

I'm sitting up straight now, holding his arms to get his attention.

– Brendan, I know this might not be fair, but I want to know where you think this is going.

– I don't know, he says, and sighs, I don't know what they think they're up to. It's scare tactics probably. Intimidation.

8

I kiss him. There's nothing else I can do. I don't let go of him for a long while.

– That's what I'm talking about, I say then, my lips glowing more than the bars on the fire. Do you hear me, Brendan?

– Aye for fuck's sake take it easy, I hear you, he says, but he's smiling, nearly laughing with embarrassment and it's that which makes me go at him again.

The summer arrived like the army once had and I went for some of those walks with him over the border, all the way by the main road to the coast or out the back ways into the hills and up to the old fort where I first felt his hands moving sorrowfully towards my breasts. The good weather gave me dreams of going away with him on holiday but he always seemed to have some excuse to do with his mother and we would put it off for another week. I met his family only once or twice—I liked the mother but the sister Majella was antagonistic from the start—while he was well known to my mother and father and even my younger brother when he was back for a week from across the water. On a few occassions we went out with some of his pals but they bored me and I failed to find their sanctimonious lassitude amusing. The two of us together, never holding hands—Brendan always refused, he was proud of his respect for the delicate sensitivities of passers-by: It's not fair, he would argue—the two of us walked the streets and the corny abundance of the old roads until the corniness itself had blossomed into something more cryptic and troubling and the hills looked evacuated for a good reason. I began to worry on some of those walks that if I wasn't careful I would become too different and unreal for him, too precious to be touched, grabbed, too pure to ever be loved. So I set about telling him all there was to know about me, show him how it was done and how easy and unimportant it was. I was always waiting for him to need me. I dreamed of it some nights, that he would turn to me and grab me and glare into my eyes with a need, the stone scalding in his throat, him raising his voice above the racket of the streets and the seething lanes, him ripping and ransacking me in the heart of the town and his laughter, cracking the lock of the skies with his laugh. At the same time I believed him when he told me he had never been as close to anyone before.

I must have been going out with him for about a year before there was any mention of Eddie. We had Brendan's house to ourselves for the first time I remember. All that day at work I felt like I was drowning and I couldn't remember where the canteen was or the toilet. I made us a dinner and couldn't eat it. Brendan was in a rare talkative mood, especially about his family, and I listened to a lot of stories I'd never heard before or expected to hear and he even leaned across the table and kissed me without being asked. The more he talked and made me laugh, the more I felt myself being taken over by a strange kind of sorrow and loneliness, about myself, then about the two of us in that room and then the streets and the houses surrounding us, so by the time we had cleared the table I wanted only to lie down with him and have his arms around me—in the dark of his room I hadn't laid eyes on yet. Brendan was too bewitched by the storytelling to notice.

– I remember one time we had this big scrap over this girl, he says, appearing in the door to the kitchen. We beat the bloody heads off each other. Then there was this other time; one night, right, we were thirteen, right and—

Who you talking about, Brendan? I ask him, mournfully. I'm sitting on the sofa with my arms around myself. He disappears back into the kitchen where he's been making us tea.

I have to follow him.

– What?

– It doesn't matter.

– Aye it does. Carry on with what you're saying. Who was the girl then? I add on, trying to sound jealous.

– It doesn't matter. He's standing with his back to me watching the kettle. There's something in his voice like anger.

– You can't get into a big huff over one question, I try saying. I didn't know who you were talking about jist.

He turns on me. Before I know it, he's right in front of me, stooping, shouting into my face.

– Jist fucken leave it. Right. D'ye hear me? Right.

I walked out of the house and the chance of our first night on a real bed. A week went by before he called at my door. I shut it in his face and told him I wouldn't have any more secrets. I thought I knew all the ones Brendan hung about with by then, most of them a shower of nail-biting corner-warmers who occasionally erupt into a night of drunken mayhem out in Dog's Forest. Another week later we went for a walk together in the cemetery and a bloodstained shirt was lying at the bottom of a new grave. He had known this fella Eddie since they were wains, Brendan told me, the wind making him even taller, his eyes blinking in surprise at the sight of the smouldering city below, they grew up on the same street, Dill Street, by the old gasworks, chased the same girls, aimed at the same soldiers, cursed the same moon. Eddie was the wilder one, the risk-taker, the wanter. His da was taken away and died in jail. Eddie was growing up with one eye already closed, Brendan said, and looked at the bare hills over the river like he was taking aim. They reached sixteen, he went on, still the best of friends, although Brendan's family had moved to a quieter part of the city. Then one day Brendan knocked at Eddie's door to see why he wasn't at school.

11

Eddie was lying in the bed but he said there was nothing wrong. The next day he wasn't at school either. At the weekend he was still lying there and saying he didn't want to go out. The following week was the same. Somehow the months went by, the streets were stripped and smashed and lobbed through the night. Brendan finished school and went on the dole. The years started to pass, unhealed and rotten. For a few hours every morning Brendan sat in the room talking with Eddie. That's where he was coming from the day we were stranded in Lilly the Crook's windowless shop.

The story about Eddie stayed in my mind for weeks afterwards. Sometimes at night I would lie awake in a state of horror at the senseless constant weight of my body against the mattress. Morose astronauts floated through my dreams and I often woke up with the sickening image of a young boy's face on an old man's wheezing body. I was also annoyed by the thought of Brendan sitting helpless and uncomplaining at the side of the whining recluse every morning for all those years. I asked did they not call the doctor or the priests or the Torchmen but Brendan just shrugged and claimed he couldn't remember any more. I was furious with his docile acceptance that the situation would never change. He even lost his temper one night when I stood up and said I was going round straight away to Eddie's house. He grabbed me and I bit him and ran to the door.

– If you go out that door . . . he said in a low voice, staring at the floor.

– If I go out that door what? I said, beginning to enjoy myself.

He looked towards me slowly and there was a stunning sadness in his face. The closer I moved towards it with my arms out to hold him, the more the sadness seemed to fade and change and become something repulsive like fear, so that by the time I was in reach the last thing I wanted to do was touch him. About a week later he told me that he had discussed the whole thing with Eddie and a time would be arranged. That would have to be done gently; he said, Eddie had not spoken to anyone other than his mother or Brendan for as long as any of them could remember.

The big day was a Sunday, dusty, bright, a young wind without a smell. Brendan called for me in a suit after mass and we walked through the streets with him talking away about the slightest thing that caught his eye, a cat on a ledge, our reflection in a window, his rumbling stomach, a boy throwing stones at the charred roundabout in the park. The house faced the big hole in the gasworks wall and a maudlin horde of rusty six foot nettles. The mother, Gertrude, answered the door, hugged the two of us like we had just returned from some long journey away and brought us into the gloomy front room which I thought at first was her bedroom because the curtains were still closed. A thick red pillar of a candle was burning on top of the mantelpiece with a flame as long as a man's finger. Brendan was surprisingly comfortable with her and even made a joke to her face which he hadn't told me about the priest at mass nearly falling over when he held up the chalice. Gertrude covered her face with her hands and shook and sniggered and stamped her foot. She is a very small woman, round and smooth like a stone on the beach, her shining knotted hair and skin the same colour, so that you don't notice the line where they meet. I was soon left alone with her while Brendan disappeared up the stairs to check out the deal as he called it. She went into the kitchen to make some tea and I sat on the sofa in the twilight rehearsing my compassion for the lonely story I was expecting to hear.

– Y'know I knew your uncle. Aye, Liam, Gertrude starts to tell me as she puts the tray down on the table between us.

Now there was a man could make a woman laugh. Like that Brendan there as well, she adds, closing her eyes and smiling. She leans over and lifts the teapot. Aw dear but I don't know what I would have done without him. Aw but he'll be a hard one to hold on to so he will aw aye.

– D'ye think so? I said a bit shocked but more amused at this description of Brendan. Then I noticed that more tea was going into the saucers than the cups.

– Shall I pull the curtains there for you so you can see what you're doing?

– Aw dear aye, that's a woman's man if there ever was one, she carries on, ignoring the curtain question. The eyes on him. Do your own milk there, love. Not like the one I had. Y'know there's some men that are so cold there's nothing a woman can do for them, you'll just never get near them. She sits back in the chair with the cup in her hand. Take a biscuit there, love. That Eddie's a bit shyer like. Aw he still thinks he's jack the lad like but Brendan's the one with the charm aw aye. Our Eddie's the type that'll fall head over heels but Brendan's always got that wee bit of a smile on him makes you think he's always only joking.

– He'll have to get himself out that room first for a start, I say, hoping to force her to say more about her son. I can't see the colour of the tea in front of me never mind the biscuits.

– Sure I know, that's what I keep telling him. He doesn't take a blind bit of notice of—Gertrude stops herself, gives a shake of her head which might mean, Don't mind me I'm jist an aul woman, and starts again in a lighter tone—Aw but sure he'll get over it. He's just sulking about something. That Brendan's always winding him up about it. Aw dear . . . She puts the cup back on the table and for the next few minutes I have to watch her giggling behind her hands in the dreary candlelit room. Aw dear, she goes on, I mind the time now

14

Brendan brought this young girl round and that Eddie locked himself in the toilet. Then Brendan gets me to pretend they're gone and Eddie goes back in to the room. So Brendan has got himself a ladder out on the street and makes the wee girl climb up and knock on the window. Aw dear it was some laugh. We thought that Eddie had dropped dead on the spot with the shock.

– But it must be hard for you like . . . seeing him up there all this time, I say, getting a bit impatient with her tolerance.

– Ack sure if it wasn't that it'd be something else wouldn't it? she says looking at me and there is even a touch of pity in her eyes for me or perhaps it was reproach. You'll know what I'm talking about when you're a mother yourself. Aw dear there's worse things love. Brendan'll fix him up one of these days with some girl or other. Sure my man was the same. You wouldn't even know you lived in the same house as him. It took him all his effort jist to get into the back of the army van. It's jist laziness with the pair of them so it is. I'm always going on to him about getting himself a wee job or something, y'know anything like a wee job in a bar or something jist to pass the time . . . a window cleaning round maybe like.

She lifted a biscuit from the plate and held it up to her face.

– What type of one is this here then? I don't like those sweet ones at all. Give me a gingersnap any day and none of those fancy tasteless things like bits of paper on your tongue.

– D'ye want me to open the curtain there so you can see?

– Naw sure you're alright love. It's not going to change the taste of it now is it, a bit of light?

Before she was finished her first mouthful, Brendan put his head round the door and gave me a look to say the big moment had arrived. I followed him up the stairs and stopped beside him outside the bedroom door wondering if I should try to seem cheerful and effortless or to appear more solemn.

Brendan turned and gave me one of the biggest smiles I've ever seen on his face, proud or embarrassed I've never been sure.

– She's ready out here, he calls in through the door.

– Alright, I hear from the other side of it.

I'm waiting for the door to be opened. Brendan elbows me.

– Hello Eddie, I say, feeling ridiculous.

– Hello.

The door stays shut.

– I told you, Brendan says, she was dying to meet you. She wouldn't give me any peace. He elbows me again. Isn't that right?

– Aye, it's all my fault.

– He thinks I'm making it up, Brendan says, smiling at me. He thinks I'm tricking him or something. Don't you?

– Naw, Eddie says.

– Y'know he doesn't even believe we're going out. Aren't we?

– Aye, I hear myself saying. We are.

– So you're working then? Eddie says suddenly, pulling on the wishbone of the conversation.

– Aye, but don't hold it against me, I tell him, doing my best to be funny. Brendan laughs but there's only the sound of the bedsprings from the room. For a second I wonder if he's getting up to open the door so I keep on talking.

– It's jist a job. It's not wile exciting or anything like. I'm one of these people who need something to do jist. I'd go off my head if I had to sit around the house all day.

I look at Brendan for his reaction. He's staring at his feet. There's the sound of the bedsprings again. I try to talk my way out of it.

– It's fine for some people. I don't care what other people do. I'm jist the kind of person who gets bored wile easily like.

16

Sure look at Brendan: he could sit and stare at the wall all day if you let him.

I elbow Brendan this time.

– Aye and who taught me that trick? Brendan goes. He steps nearer to the door and says more loudly, I wonder who taught me that trick.

– I've heard a lot about you, Eddie, I say jerking the bone back again.

– He's winding you up jist, Eddie says quickly but you can tell he's smiling. There's nothing in the voice to suggest that it is from a man who has spent the last ten years or so of his life staring at the other side of the door in front of me, a dark brown door with a newish gold handle and an overbig keyhole I was calculating if I could crouch down and look through before Brendan could get a hold of me.

– Am I now? Brendan laughs.

– I've got him under control don't you worry. I was talking to your mother down the stairs, Eddie, I say, wanting the conversation to move on.

– Eddie grabs the bone away from me. So you like music then?

– Aye, I say, confused. I look at Brendan—at his reddening neck.

– Do you then? I ask the door.

Eddie starts laughing from behind it. Brendan is grinning as well, with his hands in his pockets.

– Don't believe a word that man tells you, Eddie says.

– What? goes Brendan. Why not?

They're both still laughing.

– Jist don't, says Eddie.

– No way, laughs Brendan, it's him jist.

– Aye right.

– Aye.

17

– And who'd believe you?

– Who'd believe you more like?

That's the way it was going on between them. I tried to say something else but the two of them didn't pay me any heed. I moved in front of Brendan to catch his eye but he wouldn't look at me. I had to stand there listening to them and it was becoming more and more clear to me that they were taking the hand out of me. I went straight down the stairs and out the front door before I had even thought about what I was doing. I didn't even say cheerio to Gertrude.

Brendan caught me up at the bottom of the road under the cold shadow of the flyover. As he always did, he met my anger with silence, the head wedged back and gazing over me so that all I had to look at was the buoyant living stone in his throat, and as always, whether I was right or wrong or out of my mind, he made no attempt to explain himself or contradict me as if he had been persuaded by my anger to accept my point of view, to believe that I was talking the truth and he was blind and stupid. I told him to leave me alone and walked around the town for the rest of the day staring into the shop windows.

It was dark when I got back to the house. No one was in. My father had taken a stroke that morning and they were all over in the hospital. He was sick for months. So I had more on my mind than Eddie and Brendan after that.

In fact I might not have thought about Eddie again if it wasn't for the suicide note. I had never really appreciated the brutal bored accuracy of the name for what I read one sleeting morning with a piece of toast in my mouth on my way out the door to work.

I'm sorry. You're probably right.

By the way, we weren't trying to make a laugh of you.

18

It wasn't Eddie's fault.
I'll always remember you.
Brendan

I was half way across the town before it dawned on me what it meant. My name wasn't even on the letter. I had never seen Brendan's handwriting before. It seemed stretched and unnaturally big like he was trying to fill up the space and he had even printed his own name in small neat capitals in case I couldn't read his signature I suppose and mistook him for somebody else. I ran around to the Mc Shanes in the sleet. They had known for a full day already. Brendan's mother had also received a letter I was told but no one offered me the chance to read it or see how long it was or check for a signature. How could a person planning to jump over the bridge put down their pen and think that something so brief and incoherent was enough? For me, the best friend and lover. What was the huge rush that he didn't have time for more than twenty-five words to me? And what was I probably right about? Was he asking me to look after Eddie, encouraging me to think I should call on Eddie if I wanted more information? Had Eddie got a letter? A longer one, or did Eddie know beforehand? I pictured Eddie waiting in his room for the grieving lover to come battering down his door, in search of comfort and understanding. I swore to myself that he could sit there for another ten years if he thought I would ever give him the pleasure of showing up in that condition. I put Brendan's note in a new envelope and sent it to him. Underneath I wrote, in miniature capitals: I hope yours is longer than his.

During the months my father was sick I didn't see so much of Brendan, usually only at the weekends, and even then I was too afraid to leave the house in case something happened. Eddie was never mentioned. Brendan rarely spoke about what he did with his time and I wasn't interested enough to question him. I supposed he was with Eddie in the morning, and once they got out of bed there was Billy and Hoax and Bubble and Groover and that crowd, all disciples of the opinion that slovenliness in mind and body was the craftiest victory over the injustice of the occupying forces. It was around that time that I got myself a job as a secretary in the new radio station. The streets grew a new skin; it cracked again, allergic to hope. With the extra money I was earning, I took my driving test and bought a second-hand car from Kelly's. I started saving for the first time in my life. My father came out of danger and I began to long for a holiday somewhere, to escape for a few weeks from the house and the sarcastic piety of the skinny shrivelled streets. I wanted Brendan to come with me. He had never set foot outside the town in his life, he would declare proudly. Of course I knew it was Eddie who was behind his reluctance. Finally, in desperation, I bought us two tickets for down South, gave him one at his front door, and told him to meet me at the bus depot the next morning.

All day I sat at a plastic table in the café, watching the buses pull up outside the window and the ones getting on board and being taken away. There was one youngish lad with his head in a book, a dark and menacing face above the pages, whom I stared at for a long time, hoping he would ask me to come along with him, and I would have went no matter where he was going. I got a taxi back to the house and stayed in for a fortnight. Brendan showed up on the night of my supposed return and I had so much to tell him about my wonderful holiday and the men I'd met that he left without being able to find the time to apologise or mutely seek forgiveness which would have been more like him. He was probably expecting me to dump him that night, thought he was brave and honourable to turn up at the door to be told to his face. I wasn't going to let him off that easily.

The next few times I saw him, I made sure to keep on about the holiday while watching for portents of a looming apology but it was quickly apparent that he must have decided I didn't require one or perhaps I am giving him too much credit and he had simply forgotten about it. I thought it was all over then, that it was only a matter of time. We got through to Christmas again anyway and we were out in a Chinese restaurant on River Row trying to avoid the savage nostalgia of the pubs. Two policemen came in with four soldiers at their back. When they reached our table, Brendan refused to give them his name. They were going to take him away but I panicked and gave them the information. They still weren't satisfied and I had to beg and flirt and lie that we had just got engaged. We were silent for a long while after they went. He wouldn't even look at me.

I took his hand over the table.

– We need to do something, Brendan. If they had taken you, I jist felt that . . . I wouldn't see you again.

– I'd a been out in the morning, he says, taking his hand away.

– That's not what I meant. Then I ask him why he didn't show up for the bus.

– I had to sign on, he sighs. I did, he says again in response to the look of amazement on my face. I had my bags packed and everything. I didn't know how to get out of it. You don't understand what they're like. They don't give you any peace. One wrong move and they'll wipe you. Ask anybody.

– Why didn't you just tell me?

He doesn't answer, stares at the fork between his fingers like everything he has heard about forks is a lie and this one might easily sprout wings and fly out the door.

I say it to find out what it will feel like: I'm thinking of leaving.

– Is that what you want? he asks me like it is the sort of thing he says every day. Want is a new word for Brendan.

I laugh so loudly people look at us.

– Is this jist about the holiday? he says getting angry. I told you I couldn't get out of it. You don't know. There's a lot of things you don't know. I was stuck jist. You can't jist get up and go off whenever you want you know. Well you might. But I can't. I fucken can't jist.

I knew that all his anger was directed towards the question he thought I was asking him. The stone in his throat was burning and bulging. I wasn't sure myself whether I was asking him or not. I looked out the window at a crowd of young ones dancing in the square. Somehow his reaction would decide whether I was serious or not. I was waiting.

– I'm skint jist, he says.

I leaned over the table and kissed him. I'm not sure he realised what he had just done. That night we nearly got drunk together for the first time.

The next month and a half was our best time together, for me anyway. I worry now that I was blinded by the excitement of getting out of this place, the tear-gas of hope, that if I had paid him more attention or listened more keenly he would not have felt the need to do what he sadly did. I look back over those weeks for a strain in the smile or a flaw in the gaze or a bleeding word but there is nothing to hold on to now that the fumes have cleared. On New Year's Eve we drove over the border to the sea. We sat on the sand, not knowing if we were even facing the direction of the water, and the wind destroyed anything we attempted to say. Brendan felt restless and tense under my arm but I put it down to the cold. After a while he jumped up and grabbed my hand and we started running. There was me laughing and kicking sand as we ran along thinking we were just trying to keep warm or have a laugh. The darkness was worse running into it, huge, ancient and the wind mauling our faces. Back at the car I put my arms around him and, still laughing like an idiot, I tried to kiss him; he pushed me away and ordered me to get in the car and drive. He refused to talk about it on the way back. Something had scared him. The wind banged the sides of the car. We were stopped at the border and I swear the soldier flinched at the sight of Brendan's face in the torchlight.

On our last night out together there was another moment which might be significant or might be as important as what we had to drink. The older brother Paul had just got engaged to Mary Sweeny from the Drouth Road. There was a big crowd of us in the Mammoth. I was trapped between two old men, some bloated uncle of Brendan's and the other one with a pipe and a hair-filled ear, who either ignored each other or leaned across my legs to argue about the chronology of the events of some night long before me when a young couple went missing out the back roads and their clothes were found hanging from the trees. I was bored and at some point I was watching Brendan standing with Billy and Hoax and that lot in front of the big mirror over the fireplace. I could tell Brendan wasn't listening to the talk from the way his head was lying back on his neck like the times when we argued. Most of the bar was caught in the mirror facing him, the ones on their feet and the ones arranged around the low tables. I was wondering to myself whether he was furtively watching the scene behind him or even keeping an eye on me or if the mirror was as blank as any wall for him and he had simply lost his ability to concentrate on where he was for a few minutes. Then I saw him lick his lips. The ugliness of it almost brought me to my feet and the desire to shout across the bar, I saw you Brendan Mc Shane, I saw you, I caught you. The two old men sensed the change in me and waited suspiciously for my opinion on the vanished lovers. I sat back again in the chair and shut my eyes to escape the sight of his savouring tongue. Other than that, for the rest of the night, there was nothing uncharacteristic about him that you might expect from a man who had posted his last ever letter. I even began to enjoy myself despite his sister Majella deliberately knocking a pint of beer into my lap. I don't remember walking back with him because of the drink maybe or the wind blowing us through the streets. I can see the two of us lying on the sofa in my house and he has his hand over my mouth to stop me laughing. I can see him sitting on the floor and talking to me slowly and he runs his finger across his forehead and shows it to me for rain or dust or blood or fear. Then I am waking up the next morning in the bed with all my clothes on like a woman who was hoping to elope.

The walls of the front room where they laid Brendan out were still sticky with paint. The coffin on its stilts was as big as a bus parked between the plastic-wrapped furniture. I heard somebody say they had to slide it through the window early in the morning. I knew it was him but I found it hard not to laugh, seeing him up to his neck in white satin. His face was pale and wanton. I wanted to know what he was wearing underneath, the suit I had bought him, if he had shoes on, and underwear, but Majella never let me out of her sight for a second and made sure to fill up the room with people to make her point that I had no special rights over the body. I had never seen Brendan asleep, one eye closed with more determination than the other, the softening stone sunk in his throat. Or waking up, or naked, or singing or shaving or jumping off a bridge. There I was, a witness to his death-sodden face, but I could

24

never see a small thing like how he looked writing a letter or sitting alone in a room staring at a wall.

I went into the living room where there were more people. Mary Sweeny brought me a cup of tea and was polite enough to talk to me for a few minutes. A man was crying in the kitchen on Wee Father Pelonovitch's shoulder; he later turned out to be Devine. Three beer crates were stacked in the corner under a torn white sheet. No one made the effort to speak to me or offer any sympathy; I might as well have just stepped in off the street, attracted by the open door or the sight of a corpse. I told myself they were all unsure how to combine their grief with their shame for the woman abandoned. Maybe some of them were also asking themselves how much I knew about Brendan's suicide because in some of their looks I saw the unadorned glamour of fury.

Wee Father Pelonovitch was the only other person to approach me, took my hand and stared sorrowfully at my breasts. The wild thought went through my mind of his sleepy miniature face gorging itself on my nipple and the whole room turning in horror at the sounds of my pleasure.

– Nozing iz shir to be down untoil, he said in his wind-trapped-in-a bush accent, undzer ze eyz of ze holly. Grifz are zere to reestrain ze vanderlust. No happinezzezz.

– I know Father, thank you, I said, bowing my head, dallying with the buttons on my blouse.

Majella Mc Shane was parading herself around the room and the kitchen like it was her wedding day, demanding that everyone notice her, organising the drinks and the sandwiches and sporadic expeditions into the next room and now and again allowing herself to collapse on some embarrassed male shoulder. I'm sure she spotted Billy Richmond bravely advancing towards me across the room because she leapt on him like she was jumping off a bridge and begged him to come with her for another look at her poor flooded brother. It was while she was away that Brendan's mother caught my eye and motioned to me to join her on the sofa. I was near tears myself for her kindness. She was a very clear-minded woman, the type who believed that God's sweetest boon to women is their covert and unquantifiable suffering while it is the lot of men to fulfil their small purpose by talking themselves to death in pubs.

While I sat beside her, watching Brendan's friends sipping their cans and trying to stay awake so early in the day, she confessed to me that she had always found it strangely easy to confide in Brendan, even when he was a child, and she could only pray now that she had not laid too much on his shoulders and initiated him too deeply into the womanly quandaries of solitude. All I could do was reassure her that Brendan had a mind of his own, that he was strong and courageous and principled and that it was him who had asked me to go away with him. Although she held her huge weary head very still, I could tell somehow that Brendan had not bothered to tell her about our plans to leave. The anger went from my head to my toes and back up again where it suddenly felt more like shame, for myself, for Mrs Mc Shane, for the both of us sitting there awkwardly on the sofa at a coward's wake.

When she spoke again, it was about Eddie. She knew no more than me about the situation I was secretly relieved to hear. I told her about my visit there and talking to him through the door; she scowled and sucked her lips and shook her enormous freshly permed head. Holding me by the wrist, she confided that she had always disapproved of her son going round with Eddie and that she had even resorted to desperate measures to break them apart and how one night she had stood outside Brendan's bedroom door listening to him talking to somebody and when she barged in Brendan was lying on the bed with a grin on his face. She blamed Gertrude. She told me that Gertrude was known to wander the streets at night talking to herself. Ones said she was an informer, she had given up her own man and used the crazy act to cover herself. She also hinted that the local men dabbled with her on these ecstatic danderings and likely the soldiers as well. There's not a woman in this town will give her the time of day, she informed me, and you don't either. I was still thinking about all this when I became aware of Majella staring at us from the window, with a helicopter suspended in the creaking sky behind her like it was hers to control. Mrs Mc Shane released her grip on my wrist, which was a sign for me to get up and leave.

I went home and stayed in bed until the funeral. Wee Father Pelonovitch did it. In his attempts to find some dust to scatter on the drenched coffin, he collided with one of the uncles in the muck and dropped his book into the sagging grave. It was during the delay for the book to be recovered that Majella made her attack, coming at me from behind as you would expect. She grabbed my hair but I twisted free and, as I turned round to face her, I must have caught her across the eye with the tip of my umbrella which then flew out of my hand and landed in the grave where another uncle was fishing for the book with a spade. Majella was screaming and shouting and showing everyone what I had done to her. Her mouth was filling up with blood and rain. Gargling, she rushed at me again. I avoided it and looked for help towards the collection of soaked faces. Is there any point in repeating it? The jist of her abuse was that I was a domineering bitch who had driven her poor fool of a brother to his grave and I wasn't going to get away with it, oh no way, people would know the truth and the streets would spurn and revolt against my ugly feet.

Wee Father Pelonovitch was the first to snap out of the spectacle and stand between us to preserve what was left of our 'dignightzly'. Majella refused to go to the hospital until she had seen her brother safely in the ground out of my influence. I could have walked away but it would have looked too much like an apology or acquiescence for my liking. With the effort of standing on there among them, I don't remember much else about the service, only the same sheet of rain sweeping in front of my eyes like a magician doing the same half-hearted trick over and over again, like Brendan's eyes that first day I walked up the hill with him.

What was I supposed to do now or think? The reasons for Brendan's death were no clearer to me, but the streets and back lanes and hill roads and even my own body under the covers at night seemed to have already understood the inevitability of all things. It was in the face of this that I took to retracing some of our walks together, to the fort and out to the coast at night, struggling to convince myself that Brendan's death was a challenge to the world, to the covenant of grateful endurance, and that there was nothing inevitable about it at all. It wasn't difficult to imagine someone realising that every day was harder work than the last and being treated to some devious doodle of a resolution in the water's margin one cold unexpectant morning on the way back from the house of a hermit, but what annoyed me the most was that he had kept it all to himself, the excitement of the decision, the doubts and critical moments, the dull labour towards a conclusion that had somehow become impersonal. All those nights he sat listening to me moaning on about nothing and the cold air from under the bridge was already tempting his ankles. Was he afraid I would try to talk him out of it? Or was Majella right and I was asking too much of him by wanting to leave or simply by wanting to love him? In spite of myself, I was always imagining him in Eddie's room discussing the highs and lows of his resolve, and his guilt towards me of course, while Eddie, enthroned on his bed, kept his mind focused on higher things. Without intending to, I found myself standing outside Eddie's house a number of times, checking for some movement in the upper window, trying to keep ladders out of my mind. In a rage one morning I even knocked on the door but there was no answer. It makes me want to be sick now that I stood there in the street, shouting up at the window for him to show his face and everyone coming out of their houses to see what was going on.

I bought myself some new clothes, changed my make-up and went back to work. I saw Billy Richmond one day. He was standing outside The Chair. He would have gladly pulled his hood up and seen me walk on past with my nose in the air. I decided to stop, I went over to him and made him talk to me.

I don't know what it was I wanted from Billy Richmond. I took him back to my house and plucked the clothes off him in the kitchen. As pale as the soles of his feet, he came back that night for more and I think I must have given him too much. This went on for a few days until I was disgusted with myself and at the madness in his eyes for me. I tried to get rid of him but he would be waiting outside the house in the mornings and after work. The Devil makes work for the idle hands of the unemployed. He promised to marry me, look after me, cut off his hand, and get a job. I suppose I thought he might be able to tell me something about Brendan or even about Eddie but I was wasting my time. Brendan had committed an act beyond even the reach of his tongue and I'm sure that Billy felt he was pitying me in some way or purifying me as he plunged himself into tearful deliriums between my legs on the kitchen floor. About Eddie he was extravagantly vicious, called him poison and filth and sick and swore that if he ever laid eyes on him again it would take a legion of men to hold him back. When I questioned him further about the grounds for his distaste, he admitted that he had not exchanged a word with Eddie since they were both eleven years old but Billy was never a man to go against the opinion of the many. So I let Billy know, almost by accident of course, that Eddie and I were lovers but that I wanted to carry on with him on the side. He wasn't there the next morning. I saw him out the town once but he jumped in the door of some shop. I've heard since he was seeing Tracy O' Donoghue from the Pillars. One night she'll wake up and find him praying at the bottom of the bed for the protection of his soul.

Anyway, it was about three months after the funeral and we were walking back to this girl Christine's house who I was working with. It was just the pair of us and we were drunk as only girls can be. I was going out most of the nights then; after a lot of effort, I was pleased to discover that I had acquired a taste for the grave and svelte juice of the gin bottle—there was always one stowed under my bed for those panicked dawn awakenings. Christine told me later we were singing some song and then she looked round and I wasn't there and she went on home thinking it was amusing, for some reason, that I had suddenly disappeared. I remember looking up at a light in a window. I remember knocking on the door, maybe even kicking it with my new leather boots for the spring. I remember Gertrude answering with her coat half on and the girlish sniggering when she saw the state of me.

She led me into the front room, sat beside me on the sofa, put her arms around me and started to cry. It took me a few minutes to work out what was going on: a small old woman in a matted duffle coat was lying against me and crying and I had my chin on the scarf around her head looking at the window and the smooth unfalling stone of the moon in a bit of open sky. The same red candle was stretching and bowing on the mantelpiece as though the last six months were all a dream of mine. Gertrude was crying for Brendan and as I sat there with her I was able to understand for the first time that I would never see him again, he would not be there some day outside my door, wanting to apologise for forgetting that we were supposed to be going out together or on the street some morning when I turned a corner, embarrassed and confused and staring over my head as he listened to me questioning him about where he had been and why he had not been around.

Gertrude sat up and looked for a handkerchief in her pocket. She wiped her eyes and blew her nose and I straightened the scarf on her head with a couple of clips.

– Were you going out? I asked her.

– Aye, I was going out for a wee walk, she sighed.

– At this time?

– Aw aye I like a wee walk at night so I do, she said merrily, sure what else is there for a woman my age eh? Aw dear but, she sighed then, y'know there was one or two nights Brendan came out with me.

– Well you were right about me not being able to keep him anyway, I said, and Gertrude put her hands over her face and shook silently. I thought I heard a noise out in the kitchen, a scampering sound like the nails of a mouse tapping on the lino. I was glad I was in boots.

– Aw aye, Brendan came out with me a few times so he did, jist me and him. We had some laugh, so we did. Talking an'all. Aw aye. Did he ever tell you about it?

I shook my head, thought about being sarcastic again. Gertrude was looking up at me.

– We crossed that bloody water together y'know, she said, and she was angry now.

I wasn't sure what she meant. Turning away from me, she pulled her coat tightly around herself. She was in an old pair of house slippers, the toe almost through in one of them.

– Aw dear but he was some charmer, she was off again in a different mood. There's not many like that. These days anyway. Sure that Eddie would never come with me.

– You'd need to watch yourself out at night y'know.

She ignored me or didn't hear. Aw dear but, I remember he came running in all excited one night and he was going on about The Torchmen on the Walls and trying to get Eddie to go down and see and he'd ran all the way up to get him. That's what you call friends so you do. And then this other night too. Trying to pretend there was a fire to get him out. There was some girl in it as usual . . . aw dear the state he got himself into he almost had me believing him as well. You could nearly smell the smoke.

She hid behind her hands again. There were no rings and the hands were soft and pale and undamaged like they had never seen a day's work. I thought about Brendan Mc Shane the great lady's man, the worrier's neck, the empty eyes, the sadness in his hands. I asked Gertrude about a letter. Her head moved from side to side.

– I had to read it in the paper, she told me. Sure what is there to say anyway, she added, taking her hands away from her face. She was smiling at me.

I wanted to tell her I thought there was a lot to say, that I didn't see what there was to smile about.

– That Eddie got something, she said.

– And he didn't tell you? I was losing my temper now.

She didn't answer but the smile was still faintly on her face.

– I was talking to Mrs Mc Shane at the wake y'know.

I watched her reaction.

– Aye I knew that woman once upon a time, Gertrude sighed

and stared at the candle flame which had shrunk suddenly.

– When she was young but, she added with a note of warning. Not now. Aye, she used to go out with Bendy Hegarty, y'know the man that owns all the shoe shops?

– She was talking about you. I was annoyed now.

– I'm sure she was, Gertrude said quietly. Sure that's what it's for isn't it?

We were both silent for a while. I was looking at the moon again. It was a dead thing up there. I thought of Eddie in the room above us.

– What else could it be for? Tell me that, said Gertrude.

– You should have tried telling bloody Brendan that, I heard myself saying, almost shouting.

Gertrude sighed. Aw dear sure, Brendan knew all about that.

– I wish he had done a bit more talking to me then.

– Maybe he thought too much of you for that. I looked at Gertrude and the smile was back on her face.

– I don't understand him, I said and I was near tears myself now. He did more for your Eddie than he ever did for me. We were supposed to be going away y'know.

Did she know? Had he talked to her about it?

Her face told me nothing. Like the moon. Like his own face in the coffin.

– I don't even care anymore, I said, giving up. Why should I be the one left to figure it all out?

– There you see, Gertrude turned and smiled at me. That's Brendan for you alright. That's him all over isn't it? A charmer.

– A coward, I said.

Gertrude started laughing again. I started laughed along with her.

That's when I heard the creak of the kitchen door. I jumped up. The room was too dark to see much. I thought maybe I was imagining it again but I looked at Gertrude and she had stopped laughing and was staring in the same direction. Standing up on the sofa, I shouted at her to put on a light but she did no more than get to her feet and put her hands in the pockets of her coat like she was preparing for a long wait. I shouted at her go and see what it was. All I could imagine was a huge overweight slobbering rat nosing open the door and sticking its head into the room to see what all the laughing was about. I could hear it breathing and coughing and sniffing like it might talk. Gertrude was still standing there. I was expecting to see a rat's face coming up over the sofa and winking at me at any second. I started kicking the air around my feet and hit the table which tipped over and the teapot went flying and smashed against the hearth like a curse. Finally, Gertrude started walking across the room to the kitchen door. I told her to find something to hit it with. At the door she stopped, pulled it open quickly and reached her hand around the wall and a light came on. I calmed down a bit but stayed up on the sofa while Gertrude went into the kitchen, the door shutting behind her and leaving me again in the darkness. What is it? I kept calling to her but she wasn't answering.

Another door opened, the one out to the back yard. The moon was still up there in its own corner of the sky, the clouds afraid to touch it. In the dirt on the window I noticed a blurred handprint and scratches and smudges and near the bottom there was definitely some written words which had only been half-wiped away. I called to Gertrude again just in case and jumped down and stepped over the table to the window. The writing glowed faintly in the moonlight like it was dissolving. Along the bottom of the window Brendan Mc Shane had been practising his signature in the grime and dust. I counted eight attempts, from large confident scrawls to small ~atly joined letters as well as the gaps where he'd rubbed them out. I was suddenly terrified and ran back to the sofa because the idea occurred to me that it was Brendan or his ghost who had opened the door. Bouncing up and down on the cushions, I was even praying to him to leave me alone, not to frighten me. I was doing that when Gertrude came back in.

– What was it? I screamed at her.

– Who d'ye think? she said scornfully and bent down to the pieces of the teapot on the hearth.

– What? How do you know?

She gave me a look.

– Is he still there?

– Aye, he's out there alright.

– What are we going to do?

– Get down off the sofa for a start, she told me. Then she called out to the kitchen.

– Bring me in a brush there now will you? D'ye see the state you've got her into with your carry on? Hiding . . . and the age of you.

The door opened and in the fall of light from the kitchen there he was, long-haired, jeans and a pyjama top, unshaven like a prisoner, smaller than Brendan, a fuller build, the best-looking man I've ever seen, Eddie Mulholland.

Gertrude tidied up the hearth and went out on her walk, leaving me alone with Eddie. We talked for hours, or I did. Like Gertrude had said, he is very shy, but that makes it precious and memorable when he tells you something. He is no good in pubs or company; he needs time and close attention and when he feels comfortable you realise he has a very sharp sense of humour, too sharp at times. I laugh a lot with him but I'm not sure if he understands why. He talks to me about Brendan: he says he can't understand why and I believe him. He showed me the note he got, only fifteen words, including a printed signature and the P.S., look after her, which might

35

mean either Gertrude, which makes her giggle, or me, which doesn't surprise me.

I've seen inside his room now a number of times but we usually sit downstairs while Gertrude is out. There's a bed, a chest of drawers, a photograph on the wall of a derelict cottage at the bottom of a hill he tore out of a magazine and a window with a view of the wasteground left after they took away the gasworks which at night might be a still black sea. I've never done so much talking in my life. I go round there every night after work. We often wonder what Brendan would think about us getting on so well after all the fighting. I don't know how he would react; it deserves him right anyway after all his ludicrous efforts to find Eddie a woman. Eddie told me Brendan had made him hide behind the door that time because he thought I'd feel sorrier for him. They both got a bit of a shock when I walked out.

It was Eddie's birthday a few weeks ago, a Saturday, and I asked him to come outside with me. The rain was pouring down and there would be only a few people about I tried to persuade him. After hours of pressure from Gertrude and me, he finally agreed on condition that he could go in disguise because he didn't want any trouble or people staring at him. Gertrude and I had a great time up in the attic searching through the father's old clothes and her telling me all the stories attached to them. It was the middle of the afternoon before we were ready and there was Eddie in a cloth cap, the double-breasted green suit his father married Gertrude in, a walking stick, a pair of unused workmen's boots, and a raincoat with a felt collar dotted with fag burns from when the times he fell asleep on himself as Gertrude put it. I took him up to the cemetery to see Brendan's grave. The Mc Shanes have put up a marble cross with a heart on it. Eddie left a piece of clove rock he found in the coat pocket and I left a lipstick. We held hands and looked down over the city fading away in the mists and sweeping rain.

Mrs Mc Shane died a few months ago but I decided against going to the funeral. Majella Mc Shane married a man from over the border who ran off on her after a few months. I've seen her about a few times but we don't speak. She has a wee scar under her eye from me. My father seems to get better with every month that passes. I'm trying to talk him and my mother into a visit with Gertrude but they've heard the rumours so I doubt it will happen in the near future. I know they don't like me spending so much time around the Mulhollands but they know how I am and that nothing can stop me when I make up my mind. Around the town as well I've heard a few comments thrown at me but none of them will dare say a word to my face.

I'm not sure what happened to Devine; I was told he was dead but you can never be sure.

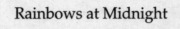

Rainbows at Midnight

I have sat here for five days since coming back from the shore, since she told me she was too afraid to go on, since I saw her last on the trampled sand look back to me in apology—and the horses had splashed her face with their slabber. I came back and wrote: *A town between two mountains is prone to the embarrassment of rainbows.* For five days I have looked at those words. I have thrown them away and written the sentence out again in different hands. I have said the words aloud at night and in the morning, in different voices, as though I might trick the silence into responding. Today I realised with horror that they equal the number of bullet wounds in her body. The streets tonight seem quiet and almost guileless, but in the distance there is the noise of a crowd.

I remember how she stumbled as she stepped down from the bus. Her arms, I noticed, hung by her sides and failed to make any movement to protect her from a fall. She was all in black again, a plain loose dress to her ankles to conceal the difficult bulk of her body. I felt an obscure obligation to lower my eyes as she made her way towards me over the uneven tarmac. Out of habit, I suppose, I thanked her for coming: usually she held out her hand to be kissed—a parody of my useless formality.

– I thought it was me who asked you to come, she said with tired sarcasm, her face turned away.

41

From the steps of the bus the driver threw the postbag across the square to another man standing in the door of a wooden hut; both men cheered when he caught it. The bus began to move off and a girl appeared at the back window and waved sorrowfully. Michelle waved back.

– I thought I was going to be late. They searched the car at the border, I said.

We walked in silence up one side of the town's main street, past the shops and arcades and florid pubs. It was still early and there were few people about. At first I was content enough to wait on her to begin talking, to tell me what was wrong and why she wanted to see me. The morning was clear and soft anyway; I remember I had to stop myself telling her about Italy, how the towns and even the villages there have ways to make you forget the brutal harshness of the sky. Michelle seemed to look at nothing around us; she moved heavily, her arms folded in front of her. She wore no make-up and her rampant dark hair which she usually kept tied and knotted high on her head—so my face won't look so fat, she used to say—was allowed to hang bleakly across her face and shoulders.

By the time we reached the end of the street I was beginning to feel impatient with her, her lethargy, her morose abandon. I knew that seeing her would not be easy, that she was in a worse state now than the last time, but I felt I deserved more than to be forced to witness her haggard resignation as though it was somehow my fault. Outside an arcade, I stopped and stood in front of her. Michelle refused to look at me. I said her name. Out of malice, I suppose, I put a coin into a machine at the door of the arcade; a pink and yellow chicken on a pedestal began to revolve slowly inside a glass cage, a siren started, lights flashed and the clucking and squawking of the machine ricocheted along the length of the street. Finally, a white plastic egg rattled into a metal trough. I offered it to Michelle, who was now wearing sunglasses; she ignored me again. Angry, I put the egg into her coat pocket and crossed over to the other side of the street.

It had been nearly a month since our last meeting. As always when we met, it was a Saturday morning, an anxious journey across the border, another gaudy heirloom town where we would not be recognised, another stretch of antique shore—the clichés of subterfuge. When she got off the bus that day Michelle was surprisingly excited and cheerful. She seemed to enjoy making me laugh. She talked to me about her family for the first time, about her mother in particular, who went round the doors selling perfume—a group of men had tried to hijack her car and so she attempted to bribe them with gifts for their wives and girlfriends, but the hooded men weren't interested. We went to look at an old watermill and then we had some lunch in a pub and Michelle continued in the same light, untroubled mood. I don't remember now why it changed—if I ever knew at all. Maybe she merely wanted to be entertaining and amusing but the effort exhausted her. Maybe she felt something or the sea darkened suddenly or a car reversed loudly up a hill. Whatever happened, she began to cry on the street.

Her nightmare had returned, she told me after a while. She had talked about this nightmare many times before, on beaches, in cafés and pubs, at picnic spots around the coast, anywhere we went, as though she was trying to keep the dream at bay. Thinking back, she was probably trying to tell me that she sensed it was already there in those places before us. This dream had appeared about ten years before when she was twenty-two and still at university. The doctors said that it was connected to the death of her father. In the beginning the dream would occur four or five times a year; each time she was paralysed for days and sometimes weeks afterwards, too frightened to go out, she fell behind in her work, lost friends and lovers, but there had been no sign of it for the last four-teen months. Now it was back. I tried my best to comfort her, told her it was naive to expect the dream to vanish altogether.

– It's not a dream anymore, she said. It's different. It won't go away. I can't go to work. I haven't been out the door in five days. I'm too scared. John won't listen to me anymore. He has to look through the letterbox before I'll open the door, so I can see his eyes and be sure it's him.

We went into a hotel bar but she wanted to leave after a few minutes. Aimlessly, we followed a road out of the town and crossed a field into some trees. Michelle was extremely quiet but she had stopped crying. The grove of birches had a floor of luminous green moss; each step brought water out of the ground. It struck me among those trees that her gloom was what attracted me to her; for the first time, I felt desire for her. I wanted to kiss her chewed and anxious mouth, wanted to undress her and kneel beside her suffering body on the bright moss. Suddenly we saw the sails of some yachts flickering through the trees.

– Colm, I think we have to stop now.

I heard her speak and said nothing. We waited in the shadow of the trees until the last taut glimmer of colour went out of sight. She took her arm back from mine and it was only then I understood what she meant.

– Maybe it's the lying. I don't know. I don't have the strength for this just. I can't go on with it.

– Go on with what? We haven't done anything.

Michelle looked at me, unconvinced.

– Is this because of the dream? An hour ago you seemed happy.

44

– Colm, I've told you so much about myself. But where can it go? Look at the state of me. I don't have any strength left. I feel like a ghost, haunting myself. And you've just come back here.

– What's that got to do with it?

– Some days it's so urgent, Colm, so urgent, she said and looked at me almost imploringly. There's this sense of emergency. I can't sleep, I can't wake up, I can't look out the window, everything is staring at me, staring at me like I shouldn't be here, like I'm an intruder. A trespasser.

She moved away and rested her forehead against a tree.

I stared at her, the heavy earrings, the hair swept up from her broad neck.

– What's so urgent about boredom? I said to her viciously. Thirty-two years of boredom. That's all that's wrong with you.

Michelle turned slowly and looked at me with distaste. She tried to laugh. There was a scrap of silver bark stuck in the centre of her forehead.

– Anything else? she said, sneering. You know there's nothing worse than cruelty in the hands of an amateur.

She walked away through the trees. I thought about going after her. I said to myself that if I did, everything would change between us, we would have forgiven and allowed ourselves to be forgiven and because of that we would learn to hate each other. I lay down on the moss and let the dark cold water soak through my clothes.

It sickens me that I've already slipped into the background story as they call it; a few hundred words and I've jumped at the chance of losing myself in what went before that last day Michelle and I spent together on the beach. What am I trying to avoid? The words themselves are afraid of her. So let's get the psychological scenery out of the way then: we met at a

film launch, moved on to a pub, we talked a lot about art—
she liked abstract work but confessed to an attraction for
Hopper. What appealed to me about her was the contrast between the graceful precision of her speech and her body
which seemed heavy and a burden to her. At the end of the
night, I was walking home in the same direction and she invited me in but not before she informed me, with a laugh, of
her nuptial contract. The husband, John, however, was out of
the country for the weekend. We were both drunk but nothing happened between us. A sum of six times we met after
that first night when she fell asleep on the sofa half way
through a story from her wild days at university and I left,
slamming the door diabolically behind me to attract the
neighbours' attention. She had exhilarating green eyes, she
was revolted by the touch of velvet, an insomniac, she often
described herself as a socialist, she worked as an art teacher,
she was overweight, she claimed to have a powerful sense of
smell, she had once spent a week alone in Berlin, she wore too
much jewellery. I never slept with her and I don't think I
wanted to.

I left Michelle with the plastic egg in her pocket and walked
up the other side of the street. After a few minutes, I turned
round and saw her still standing outside the arcade, her head
bowed at an awkward angle. Two women hesitated on the
pavement before feeling safe enough to pass her. I watched
her for a time, long enough to smoke a cigarette, standing
alone and stooped on the bright morning street. I went back
to her and she touched my hand.

– I can't move, she whispered to me.

We sat in a small café, in the back of a bakery. I had never
seen her so depressed. I took the sunglasses off her and she
stared at the table, the coffee cup, the saucer, the silver tail of the

spoon. She picked up the spoon and held it between her joined hands. Her nails were tended, I remember noticing, mauve and glossed. I began to feel anxious but I tried to keep myself from asking her futile questions, hoping that she could find some way to talk to me. Late the night before, she had rung and asked me would I meet her; she needed to talk to someone. I resisted the urge to mention her husband's auditory duties. She wouldn't say what was wrong but she wouldn't hang up either, so for almost an hour I listened to her breathing, the jangling earrings and bracelets when she moved, and the insinuating hum of a helicopter over her house. As I was assuring her I would see her the following day, my own room was filled suddenly with the blank, rigid beam of the searchlight.

– It's my anniversary today, I said to her, attempting to be whimsical. I'm back eight months today.

Her eyes closed as she tried to make a smile. I looked at her big face, the mouth, the swollen cheeks, the exhaustion.

– Michelle. Tell me what's happening, I said and wished I hadn't.

I waited on her eyes to open. She sighed, I think. I felt something like panic stir in me, sitting there with a woman who didn't want to open her eyes anymore. The thought went through my mind that in ten years' time this closed, sombre face would wake me up in the night. A waitress passed our table, smiled at me, and I looked at my hands in shame.

The waitress was a girl of about eighteen, with a freckled face and arms and long straight hair. She lifted a cake from the counter shelf and settled it into a white box she had assembled. An old woman entered; she used a walking stick, a metal one, and wore high-heeled shoes. The waitress leaned over the counter and the old woman whispered into her ear. The girl shook her head, frowning, and glanced out of the window to the street where two men with their sleeves rolled

47

up were talking—or it may have been at the shutters going up on the chemist's opposite.

– Is that interesting?

Michelle had turned round to see what I was looking at. When I finally caught her eye, she was almost spitting at me with anger, or worse.

– I should warn them, shouldn't I, Colm? Don't you think you should ask their permission first? If you're going to steal them and order them about and fit them into some story and they can't do a thing about it. The girl all freckles and disappointment. The old woman who's lost all her fine sons to the cities of glass. Should I warn them, Colm? You could have them blown to pieces and they couldn't stop you.

She laughed mockingly when she was done and sat back in her chair. I looked at her, wondering how to react. Michelle was attacking me for some reason: she was well aware that I had written nothing since coming back, that I spent my days in bed to avoid facing myself and the emptiness.

– It's you that'll end up in a story if you're not careful, I said, trying to be both funny and threatening.

Michelle seemed to have lost interest in the argument already. In a hollow voice she said: It's better though. She looked quickly at me: Even the urgency has gone now you know. It's calm now. No alarms. I even slept last night after I talked to you.

I finally asked her why she wanted to see me.

– Just to tell you, she said. That last time, I felt embarrassed after telling you all those things. I shouldn't have. It's a lot better now.

– And that's all? I asked, still with a touch of resentment.

For a moment, as we stared at each other, I thought I could see that she was on the verge of telling me something, that what she wanted to share with me was painfully crawling its way up through her body into her mouth. I waited, in dread and disgust. Then, almost to my relief, I saw her close her eyes and shake her head in defeat. I know now that she was trying to say goodbye to me.

The sky had clouded over when we came out of the café, although there was no wind. The day seemed fainter, tenuous, failed already—or maybe that was just my own feeling. Without speaking, we headed slowly out of the town towards the beach. It was my turn now to feel the despondency in everything and it was an effort to keep walking; inexplicably, the soles of my feet started to hurt. I didn't dare look at Michelle, I was too afraid of being dragged down deeper into her gloom. I remember the way the hem of her dress floated and flapped morosely against her boots. I remember the torment in imagining the hand that had pressed the thousands of seashells into the cement of the walls all along the road.

We turned a corner and there was the water, as it always is, grieving and bloated with piety. Men were building on the pier. A set of iron steps led down to the pale sand and the ornamental barricades of dunes. Up ahead of us, two women were playing with a dog in the foam, there was a group with a ball, and in the far distance, where the beach ended at the golfcourse wire, there was another group of people, some of them on horseback. Michelle paid no attention to any of it and took up her martyrish position at the edge of the water, the clotted foam piling up around her boots. A brown mist was gathering out over the water and it sluggishly drifted towards us, like some breath from an extinct world, until it concealed the thin crust of land across the lough.

– I always thought this was the sea, Michelle said. When I was young. I don't remember seeing any land.

As she spoke a rainbow appeared behind the men working on the pier. I left her admiring it and walked up the sand towards the dunes. A girl on a horse pounded along the beach as far as the footballers. I sat down and watched the weary figure of Michelle with the heraldic rim of the rainbow behind her. I felt myself pitying her and at the same time hating her for being so helpless, so wretched. What was wrong with her anyway? She had more than most people—a job, a house, a future if she wanted. What was she doing messing about with me? I was useless to her, and to myself; I couldn't even write anymore. I began to think about my anniversary again, the last night I had spent in Rome, on Valeria's crumbling balcony. Suddenly, the reasons for coming back here were gone. Or maybe I didn't have a reason for coming back and there was no suddenness about it. What was I looking for by returning? I asked myself. I couldn't remember. I didn't know if there was anything to remember.

It was raining lightly when Michelle sat down beside me. She was shaking and I could see she had been crying. She scooped a hole in the sand and took out the plastic egg; then she buried it, smoothing the damp sand with the back of her hand. I was tired, pretended I wasn't interested, said nothing.

– John left me, she said quietly. After a long silence she went on: I need help, according to John. Living with me is like a punishment for a crime, according to John. He's afraid of me and he says my bed must be what hell is like. He's probably right too.

– Come off it, I told her. You'll make yourself into what he sees. Don't think like that.

– There's no point fighting it, Colm. I'm just waiting now.

– You kneel down long enough and you'll start to believe, I said, annoyed, at her, and at myself for sitting there beside her on the drizzled-on scrap of shore. But the desire to be somewhere else filled me with more disgust than remaining where I was.

Just then, there was a fresh reeling brightness amongst the clouds and the rainbow returned. Beside it, almost touching it, another rainbow appeared, a fainter, trembling one which vanished and then came shivering back, faded again into the swelling mist while the men on the pier pushed planks through an electric saw. To distract her, and myself, I told Michelle about a night in the north of Norway, long after midnight, when the sun and moon were in opposite corners of the sky, it began to rain, and a rainbow appeared. I wrote a story about it, I told her and talked my way through an imaginary scene with a girl and a pack of hunters in the woods. Whether or not she was even listening—it didn't really matter—she said she wouldn't mind reading it. I had to tell her it had got lost somewhere, on the move from one city to another, I said. I even went as far as speculating where the story might be, invented a friend, a pair of thieving hands.

– Colm, what am I going to do? Michelle interrupted me, grabbing my hand. I was thinking on the bus that maybe I should go away. Maybe it's just this place and I'll feel different if I'm somewhere else.

Before I could answer, she shook her head again as if she was admitting it was impossible.

– I don't know, Michelle.

She looked defeated. The two women with the dog passed by along the water's edge. A mother and daughter, I thought. They waved to us. The dog came running behind them, a stick between in its mouth, watching us. Up the beach I noticed that the footballers had gone home.

– There's nothing urgent here, I said to Michelle. We're just sitting here on the beach and we're going to get soaked.

Maybe because I wasn't sure what I meant by that, I put my arm around her. Her back was broad and solid—too big for me to comfort, almost repulsive. I held her hand instead, turned the assortment of rings on her fingers to release the wedged sand.

– I shouldn't be doing this to you, Michelle said.

It was another of those moments when it was up to me to speak if I wanted to keep her. I did not want to be responsible for her, to step in now that the husband was out of the way. I was tired of her and her great unliftable sorrow. When she stood up, I saw the sand clinging to her boots, the lank hem of her dress and a line of horses galloping up the beach, veering into the water and along the base of the dunes.

– Colm? I heard her saying.

I kept my eyes on the horses; didn't answer. She waited for something more. I heard her mumble to herself.

When she turned away, she walked blindly into the path of the horses. The riders shouted and pulled on the reins to avoid her, trying to go either side of her. The horses seemed to scream: most managed to pass her, but not without Michelle feeling their breath and the brush of their flanks. One hit her hard and she fell on her knees on the trampled sand. The riders regrouped further along the beach. For too long, Michelle stayed on her knees, and I did nothing at all, made no move towards her. She got up. One of the riders was running in her direction. Michelle looked around at me with a look of profound apology. Her face and hair were speckled with horse phlegm. The rider gave her a handkerchief and they walked up the beach together towards the others. Before I left, I dug up the egg—it was empty. She must have opened it and kept the contents. Or thrown them away.

This morning I heard on the television that Michelle was

dead. They showed images of the street where she had been hit by a spray of bullets intended for a passing army jeep: Michelle was hit twelve times while the jeep escaped unscathed. The reporter described the deceased as a local woman who was married without children. An eyewitness said they didn't notice the woman on the ground for a few minutes after the shooting had stopped. I know the street well but it took me some time to recognise it because the camera was looking down from an unusual height, a tragic elevation, from a window or the roof of a television van. Next there was a series of close-ups of people looking dubiously at the segregated space on their street, as though it was the ground itself that had made her a victim. Then there was an aerial shot of the city from a helicopter.

A town between two mountains is prone to the embarrassment of rainbows. When the bell is rung in the town square, it is a common sight to see people drop what they are doing or abandon a conversation on the street to run indoors. Strangers arriving in spring-time often complain of feeling unwelcome.

Curfew

There were four other men in the room apart from his Da and his big brother Eamon. They were all finishing off their cans of beer, not talking. It was cold and some of them were still wearing their coats. With the curtains left open, the room was darker than the street but nothing was moving out there. Fergal could see as far as the corner where The Frankie and the rest of that crowd used to hang about before all this started.

– Glad you're back then?

That was Mr Harley's voice, only you couldn't be sure which one he was of the shadows in the dark room. His Da was the one near the fireplace. Eamon was a dead cert with the wagging leg on the sofa. There was a sigh from his big brother which could have either meant yes or no, and he raised the can and dipped back his head to drain it.

– It's always hard.

Eamon crushed the tin in his hand. There was some laughing. His Da was laughing too loud.

– Did you come to that conclusion on your bed Fluff or some other place of permanent repose? Mr Deaney said. Mr Deaney always spoke as if he thought he was at a funeral. Mr Harley was laughing as well. Fergal didn't know the man Fluff. The laughing stopped when Eamon struck a match and their faces appeared and their shadows stretched up the walls.

His Da got out of the chair and stood in front of the fireplace. He took something out of his trouser pocket and left it on the mantelpiece. He put his hands behind his back and sighed and shook his head. This was a room for important occasions. There used to be ornaments in the glass cabinet under the window. No fire was ever lit in the grate.

– Go and fucken ask wee Jimmy Glyn if you want to know about doubt.

That was his Da, like he couldn't keep it to himself any longer.

After a while Mr Deaney said, almost whispering, We can't be sure, that's all I'm trying to say. Nothing more.

– Who the fuck else would do it? Tell me that one, his Da answered straight away.

– There's no other way of thinking about it, Mr Walsh said from the chair in the corner. Mr Walsh sang at mass some Sundays with his eyes closed.

Mr Deaney stayed quiet. In the dark his Da made noises of disbelief. Mr Harley leaned forward and put his elbows on his knees. The man beside Eamon changed his position on the sofa a few times.

– Sure who knows anything for sure? If you ask me, some things are impenetrable and we'd be in some state if they weren't.

That was Fluff again.

– Our Fergal's laughing at you there, Fluff, Eamon the bastard came out with. He's sitting there and he thinks it's wile funny what you jist said.

– Is he now? Fluff said, pushing himself up to the edge of the sofa.

– Leave the wee fella alone, went Mr Deaney's voice.

– Aye, and that's another thing, James, Eamon went on to Mr Deaney. Y'know this wee brother here of mine. Well, I've been hearing stories about him and your wee girl Nuala. They're a big item from what I've heard. Always hanging about together and sneaking off y'know like. You'd need to watch him so you would.

His Da let out a big roar like it had come down the chimney and that was the sign for them all to start shouting and cheering. Fluff clapped his hands like it was the first time he had learned. Mr Deaney put his fingers in his mouth and made a whistle. Eamon threw the squashed can across the room at Fergal's head.

He went out of the room and up the stairs. Behind him, his Da was calling and them all laughing and whistling. Fergal sat on the bed and put his feet into his boots still soft from the polishing he had given them the night before. No way was he staying in now whoever was giving the orders. All day dobbing around the docks he wished he had gone to school instead of having to listen to Harkin going on about the big slaughter and the spoils. He was glad when he got home and lay down on the bed and he must have fallen asleep with his coat on. He woke sweating. It would be a better laugh to stay in he decided, with the house all to himself, and he could wait for them to come back to hear the stories. There would probably be a crowd and he could stay up late listening to the stories and maybe he'd be slipped a tumbler of whiskey. Fuck all that now. He was going out this night and it was their bloody problem if he was caught or kidnapped by whoever it was.

He put a knife down his boot and went over to the window to watch for the men leaving. The black sky seemed to slant down into the street. Stars crawled up it. The lights were out in the houses along the street except Downey's where the da gave out marbles up the town and called them gifts. The men's voices came up through the floor; they were arguing by the sound of it. Thinking again, Fergal took off the boots and pushed them under the bed. He went back to the window. A few nights before he had been standing in the same spot when Walker and two men called at the door. Walker had the dogs with him. His Da was out of his sight in the doorway, apart from his arm that stuck out once and pointed up into the sky. Walker did most of the talking and he patted the dogs on the head. Fergal went down the stairs and asked who it was but his Da started shadow boxing and laughing and Fergal got a bad punch on the ear.

The bedroom door opened and Eamon was there with one arm in his coat. Fergal kept his back to him and tried to stare at the snapped lamp-post at the corner like it was his own staring that had the power to break it. Eamon said something and pulled the zip up on his coat.

– You going to be a good wee boy then? You huffing?

– Fuck off, Fergal mouthed silently to the window.

– Don't you fucken move out this house. Right. You hear me?

Fergal turned to face his brother. You think you can jist come back and . . .

Eamon stared him down. Aye I do, he said.

– I hope somebody knocked your head off one night.

Eamon did his sarcastic laugh and put up his fists for a mock fight.

– Put on your pyjamas now wee boy, he said, and I'll be back in a while to read you a story. Once upon a time there was this wee shithead who didn't listen to what his big brother told him. You can make the rest up yourself.

Running through the streets at night, with the curtains flicking open in the blacked-out houses, like he was charging the darkness itself, Fergal let a scream out of him which made the hair on his neck move. A dog howled back and he screamed again. A man in a vest appeared at a window who was the da of that wee lad Brown who was always too sick to come out of the house. He picked up stones on the move. He took aims and drew back his arm at an old cooker in the street, a lamp-post, the window of an empty house, a car door in a tree, some shape at a corner, a beer keg, a coat lying over a gate and launched stones at the darkness itself.

Outside a group of three wrecked houses which stood alone above an embankment, he gave the whistle, like the sound of a bomb dropping. Harkin didn't answer. He climbed in through a window hole and whistled again and then he moved into the next house through a gap in the wall and looked up at bony rafters all pointing to the same spot in the sky where there was nothing. The third house had a roof and half of the upper floor but you had to climb up the back of the chimney to get to the supply of weapons and blankets stored up there. He drifted back into the middle house and sat on a mound of bricks under the rafters which were like hands about to pray. No matter what Harkin said, it was safer on the ground and easier to escape if somebody came after you and you wouldn't be cornered. Up above you were stuck and had just to wait if you heard a noise and grip your wee knife and hope and it might be something you'd have no chance of tackling all along.

It was the same in the hut. A twig breaking or a rustle and you had to charge out and attack, not just sit there holding your breath and hoping like Harkin. Huts are for hiding, Harkin always says. They are invisible under the ground. That's the point of them. Nobody will find you if it's a good hut and the ground's well camouflaged. Fergal believed most of this was right but you would never know if it was a bad hut until it was too late. A hut is about the person or thing outside being as afraid to come tearing in as you are to rush out. But what if they didn't have the same fear? And the things without fear? There might be things without fear.

It must be more than two months now since they were both

down there the last time. The hut was in a clearing behind the trees and bushes on Hunch Lane. This was the biggest hut they had built and there were different rooms with walls made out of muck which they smoothed flat and candles and carpet they found near the reservoir. The roof was corrugated sheets from a shutdown pub, supported by bricks and stakes of wood and they replaced the sods on top of it in the same order they were cut. They carried bramble bushes from out the back roads and covered the entry.

That last time was just before all the trouble started and they were drinking a bottle of cider and Harkin was talking about what he was going to do with his life as though it mattered and Fergal was listening and asking himself why he never thought about questions like this. The bottle got emptied and Harkin shut up for a while. They heard laughter outside the hut then. Right outside the entrance, and moving across the roof above their heads where the bramble was packed tight. Harkin grabbed him by the arm to wait.

The laughter went on and on without fading or getting louder. A midget man out walking in the dark, laughing away to himself for the sake of it—that's what it sounded like. Harkin whispered something and shook his head at the same time not to chance it. Fergal elbowed him out of the way and threw himself towards the opening and screamed with the knife out. He stood up in the brambles swiping his knife and there was nothing to be seen. It was quiet. Harkin crawled out with a sewer rod. A moon was up and nothing was escaping though the brambles and trees. They waited and watched for a long while and then they walked home without talking about it. Fergal went into the backyard and looked in the window and he saw Eamon had come back and he was sitting in the chair near the fire with his coat still on.

Now, squatting on the bricks in a roofless house, he heard

a girl's voice say his name. The face of Nuala Deaney was looking in at him through the window hole.

– You were dreaming.

– I was like fuck.

– I could have got you there.

– What you doing out?

– Same as you, she said. Enjoying myself.

She disappeared from the window and Fergal dragged his feet through the bricks on the floor and jumped out into the street after her.

– Does your da know? he called to her.

– Does my da know what?

– He was round at ours.

– I wouldn't put it past him.

Nuala Deaney was still in her school uniform which they called a pinafore with a baseball cap on her head and her ponytail pulled through the space in the back. The cap was new. IHS was written along the front in white letters and he wanted to ask about those letters. He watched her skim some broken slates over the wire. She picked up a bit of wood.

– So did you hear? she started to question him, flipping a stone into the air and batting it over the wire that ran down one side of the embankment. About the cows up on the hill? WACK. Drained all the blood out of them. And that wee girl WACK in the stream? They—shite—I thought you'd be with your Eamon.

– He's a fucken bastard jist.

– So do you think WACK it's the gypsies or not?

– It has to be. Dead cert.

– Why? She turned to look at him.

– Who else is it going to be? Aul Mrs Kerrigan like? He pulled himself up on the windowsill.

– Harkin WACK doesn't think it is.

– Does he? He didn't say that to me. He's showing off jist. And where is he now the slabber?

WACK.

Fergal watched the stone vanish into the darkness like that was where it belonged all the time.

– Is your Eamon—shite—going to stay then?

– Fucken hope not.

– Shite, that's two in a row.

– Not a good sign, Fergal said. I wouldn't chance another one.

– I have to, Nuala said, but as she was searching for the right stone they both noticed the movement of lights among the trees away out across the fields they knew were there in the darkness. Fergal jumped down off the window and walked over to the edge of the embankment. They watched the lights. Nuala threw the bit of wood up into the air and neither of them moved when it landed behind them among the old slates.

The tall wooden gates into Frederick Farm were tied back to the trees. Torch beams flashed and lopped and swiped through the dark and the trees and the muck and men's faces at all angles. Cars and vans made a line on each side of the lane. Up ahead, a tractor stood in the greenish light from the open farmhouse door. Fergal thought he had caught a glimpse of his Da at the front of the crowd. He heard Mad Hugo's laugh before he spotted him, along with Eamon, drinking from a bottle. Slanty was looking down at the muck, probably worrying about his shoes and wondering whether to give his hair a quick comb before the action. There were many faces and cars he didn't recognise.

Nuala wouldn't stop talking no matter how many times he told her. He gave up waiting for Harkin at the houses and ran across the fields, followed by Nuala talking and trying to be stupid by falling over or pretending she'd broken her ankle. The crowd was faced towards the gates and the farmhouse so the two of them hid behind a shed at the back. The branches lay on the shed roof like they were exhausted. Nuala scraped the moss off the corner of the shed with her bangle. She was saying something about Harkin now.

Harkin was a mouth. After all his talk about the spoils, he was too scared to sneak out. He was always making plans he never stuck to. If Harkin went to the shop for you, he came back with something different and if it was his idea to cut brambles out the back roads, he'd dander off and start fishing with his hands in a stream.

– Well that's what he told me, Nuala was saying. That there was this girl and she came to your hut some nights.

– Our hut?

– Naw, aul Mrs Kerrigan's. Harkin told me she was older and he didn't know who she was.

– A girl?

– She might have been a gypsy for all he knew, that's what he told me.

– He's a fucken mouth. When like? Sure we haven't been down there in ages. He's fucken slabbering so he is.

Nuala hissed at him to keep his voice lower.

– He's a fucken lying bastard.

– Maybe you weren't there.

– What? I'd know jist. Sure what's a girl going to be doing in our hut? He's making it up. He is.

Nuala was pointing now.

– He's jist making it up, Fergal went on. Sure where is he now and he wouldn't shut up all week?

Nuala elbowed him.

Four men were coming down the path from the farmhouse. One of them held a torch aimed at the ground. The crowd

65

went silent and closed together and their torches were lowered, lighting up the legs in the muck and the sky and trees went darker. The four men stopped at the gate as if it was the edge of a cliff. The crowd waited way below. The one in the hat who was definitely Walker took a step forward over the edge the same as on Sundays when he stood out in the aisle with the collection baskets or was coming towards you with his hand out to tell you to stop talking. The dogs followed him. Half Kerry Blue and half greyhound. They hung and cowered at his heels like things that knew they were strange and beyond pain and they sat upright in the muck with their ears pointed to the sound of his voice.

– How are we the night boys? Smell the soil on the air, boys. The aroma of solitude. Black honey. Drink it in, boys. The heart aches and the blood burns to be at peace. Even the animals know this. Even an animal knows the time to act. And bear in mind there are ones at home tonight, men with nothing to do. We have sat around for long enough, watching the shadows cross the windows, listening to the scratchings behind the door, where there is no window and where there has never been a door. We have all been hiding, boys. Hiding our heads in the sand. But fear is no compass. There is no map for the wilderness before us. What does the soul call out across the wilderness?

– I'm thirsty, Mad Hugo let him hear. Some of the crowd laughed and the talking swelled and ceased suddenly.

– Very true, said Walker, shifting the brim of his hat. But we need clear heads, boys, not moonshine. Not the wildness of men who do not even recognise their own front door. The faces of friends. Where is the moon tonight, boys? The moon is the light of fools and cowards. The dream of men without a home. But bear one thing in mind, boys: they are not afraid of us. Do not break off on your own. I want us all to go home to our beds tonight and sleep without regret or shame. Now, before I hand you over to Frederick here, I would ask that young lad over yonder, maybe two of them, to step out from behind that shed and show himself. Or on their own heads be it.

With the words a hundred torch beams seemed to grab hold of them among the trees. For a few seconds there was only a blazing light in the world like it must have been at the very beginning of things. Fergal looked into the glare and wondered at the sense of having seen it before. He thought he heard his name said. Hurried streaks of lights broke away from the bright source and then he heard voices. Even then, he might not have moved out of the path of the lethal wands if he had not recognised his brother's voice near him. He ran for it. Keeping low, he made it through the trees and across a path into bushes and through the long grass at the edge of a field. He remembered Nuala. All he had to do was keep out of sight for long enough and they would give up in case they missed the action at the farm. He wondered if they had got Nuala.

Eamon was the first out into the field, slashing the torch around like a sword, across the ground, the trees and up into the sky. Someone else limped out next who was Mad Hugo. Eamon ran further on into the field, slicing and stabbing the dark with the torch. Mad Hugo shouted. Eamon was moving in circles. Mad Hugo shouted again and headed back into the bushes. Fergal watched his older brother kick the ground. He put the torch under one arm and cupped his hands around his mouth. If that's who I think it is, you're dead meat, wee brother.

Fergal closed his eyes in the long grass and laughed. Whatever happened when he went back to the house, who caught him, what punishments, even if the worst gypsies got their hands on him, it wouldn't matter because they would never be able to beat the image out of him of Eamon in the dark field jabbing with his torch. Since that night in the backyard when he saw Eamon sitting there with his coat still on, the house seemed to grow bigger and bigger like a castle you couldn't find a way out of. The rooms were so big you had to whisper. He went in and he could tell from the light and the air that Eamon and his Da had been sitting there for hours without a word. The thing was, Eamon didn't seem to be changed by being away. Four years should do something to you. Fergal had always imagined his brother in big cities crowded with people and noise. Sometimes he hoped they would hear about his death in mysterious circumstances and everyone would ask him and no funeral was possible. He searched his brother's face and his accent and his clothes and under the bed and followed him about the streets and waited outside pubs and in rooms with him for some sign or mark or bit of evidence of a story. His brother might as well have been living under the ground for those years. Even the ornaments on the mantelpiece changed over the years. The wall around the backyard was different. Even a man in jail has a story to tell. He asked his Da and his Da said, You jist get sick of it. It's only yourself you're kidding.

He ran towards a paler patch in the dark where he could see through the high branches to the stars. The heavy whiffs of pine stung his eyes. He was sweating already and the sweat smelled of the pine and took it under his skin. He was working towards the reservoir. When he circled back to the farm, he found the cars in the empty clearing, the gates closed and the footprints in the muck filling with water and reflecting the stars. He climbed through bushes into wet mossy ground and on into a grove of ferns and up a slope on the trunk of a tree to a stony area where a foundation pit had been dug in the past and the cement powder was hard in the bags.

Still there were no voices or signs of people. He looked back but there was nothing to see. He found himself wishing he had stayed in the house like he wanted and waiting for them to come back to tell him all about it. He ran on to put a stop to the thought. Near where the stream should be, he halted and lay down on the hollow-feeling ground.

Over on the right, he saw a shaking glow between the columns of the trees of a fire about a good stone's throw away. For a long while he watched for movement. The fire was weakening in a ring of stones. The ground around was stirred up and scattered like there were plenty of feet. Somebody had taken a piss against a tree. Lifting a hot stick, he sifted through the pieces in the fire. Deep in the ash, he turned something over and hooked it clear to get a better look. He was a long time finding it again. He kicked the smoking thing back towards the light of the fire and saw it was a blackened skull and hairy with cinders and needles.

He dropped the branch and knife and ran, trying to listen past the thumping of his feet for another sound in pursuit of him. To the left, he saw a barbed wire fence with a slope down to the overflow basin. Straight ahead were trunks of different sizes and some had fallen into the arms of others. Beyond that leaves whipped his face. He went over a hidden wall and found himself surrounded by nettles taller than him. He pulled the jumper up over his face and charged in.

At the brambles he stopped. He was running without a notion of what he wanted and he knew that was a mistake. He told himself to think. He could try the hut or get back out on to the path and head for the farm along the lanes. There were weapons in the hut they had never collected. The sky was greener now, the stars grey. He made a move for the hut and stopped. He let a shout out of him because he couldn't decide. While the shout was still in the air, the back of his knees caved in and he dropped forward into the brambles. A boot to the arms brought him face down into the scalding thorns and hooks. Another one under the ribs made him wretch. He saw his Da looking up into the morning sky and a bird flying past with a clump of his youngest son's hair in its bloody beak. He saw Eamon chasing burning dogs around the streets with bits of his brother tied to their tails. Harkin and Nuala hid his tongue in a box under the bed and Harkin told her stories about the gypsies.

– Sweet mother of fuck I didn't know it was you, Fergal hi. You alright? Fuck me I hadn't a clue who it was. That shout just scared the life out of me.

That was Mad Hugo's voice.

A boot turned him over and the light slammed into his eyes and the cuts.

– I fucken warned you didn't I eh? What the hell are you up to ya wee fucker?

So Eamon was there too.

– Who is it? said Slanty from further away.

– It's wee fucken Fergal so it is, said Mad Hugo. I nearly killed him the wee man.

Eamon knelt on his chest and put the torch in his face.

– What the fuck you up to?

– I can't see. Move the torch.

– I don't give a fuck. What are you up to?

– Is he on his own?

– I don't know, Fergal tried to tell them. I can't see with that in my eyes. I was over in the forest. There was this fire.

– Who were you with in the forest?

– I don't know. There was this fire and then I ran over here to the hut and—Fergal got a slap on the side of the head.

– What hut? Eamon said.

70

– In there. Move the light.

Eamon's mouth was right against his ear now. Y'see if you're up to anything, y'see if you are wee bro, I'm going to beat your head in non-stop for a fortnight.

It went dark and he lay there on his back listening to the three talking. They had chased somebody into the brambles. Slanty wanted to give up and find the rest. Eamon was all set for staying. Mad Hugo told him to take it easy. Slanty wanted reinforcements and Eamon told him to wise up. They were carrying crowbars.

Mad Hugo pulled Fergal up to his feet and slapped him on the back.

– You'll be alright wee lad.

Fergal touched the blood on his face. He sniffed the pine smell from the blood on his finger.

– Who else knows about this hut then?

– Nobody. Me and Harkin just.

The torchlight hit him in the face again.

– What about our wee Nuala?

– Naw.

– Y'sure? Where is she the night then?

– I don't know. I can't fucken see.

– And nobody else knows.

– Naw. I haven't showed it to anyone anyway.

– Just you and Harkin and nobody else ever set foot in it?

– Naw. Harkin might of but I didn't.

A hand gripped him by the neck. Eamon's face was there in front of him.

– Harkin might of what?

– I don't know.

– Harkin might of fucken what?

– He said this girl knew about it but he was only fucken lying. He was just making it up.

71

– What girl?

– I don't know.

– Say I don't know again and I'll ram this down your throat.

The cold claw of the crowbar touched his swollen lip.

– I fucken don't. He said he didn't know her either. He was jist fucken slabbering so he was. He said it was this gypsy girl but he—

Fergal felt himself falling backwards into the brambles again. He couldn't tell where he had been hit, in the stomach or across the head. Eamon was battering the brambles with the crowbar. Mad Hugo said he knew all along it was a girl they had seen. Fergal thought of the old kings burned on the top of bonfires. He thought of boats on fire crossing the horizon. For every star there was a cut in his face. He was floating on a cloud of burning brambles. He closed his eyes and drifted like smoke across the fields and through the streets.

They made him stand up and told him he was going into the hut to see who was there and any funny business and they would strip the skin off him. Fergal asked for a torch but Eamon stopped Mad Hugo handing him one. They wouldn't give him a weapon to protect himself. He felt a jab from the crowbar between his shoulders and he stepped forward through the brittle cloud at his feet. He saw the underground rooms of the huts and the smoke filling the dark if he didn't come out again. But what if it wasn't empty and this girl was inside? Maybe there was a mad horde of them in there. Harkin might be involved with it and that's why he had told Nuala as a sort of warning. Fergal looked back at the three of them and a light struck his face. One of them spoke, probably Eamon. What if it was them? Eamon might be in on it. Where was everybody else? Eamon came back around the time it all started. They must bloody know already who was in there.

He sucked in his breath for the pain and made a jump to the right and ran towards the gap in the hedges. He knew exactly where it was. They were after him straight away. Eamon was shouting. Mad Hugo laughed. There was a low strip of barbed wire you had to avoid. Another jump and he landed in the ditch and crawled out of there into the lane on his hands and knees. He slid back in again and gripped the grass to pull himself out. His brother landed in there behind him just as Fergal made the path again. Another light exploded in his face and a boot pressed him down into the muck. He was ordered to stay very still and he lay feeling the cold muck against the hacked face. A dog was growling. Above him he could hear the low voices like these were men meeting any night on the street under his window. Something sharp with a thick point scraped the side of his neck but it wasn't metal. Then in his ear an animal panted and sniffed up his smell.

– What's the joke there, Paddy?
  – Talk about half hung.
  – You could see right through.
  – Some handful.
  – What's the word for it?
  – I missed that bit.
  – More's the power to him.

Nuala was sitting beside him on the floor with her knees up. Her hat was lost. He had some whiskey in a tumbler from Mad Hugo. His Da started off being against any drink but then he forgot. When he sipped it, the cuts stung on his lip and up his face. Nuala wanted him to go into the hall with her or up the stairs to tell him something important she said. Imagine them all laughing and jeering if he went out of the room and Nuala behind him. He couldn't tell her that. Harkin

73

was looking at him and trying to wink at him from the other side of the room, on the scran for butts. With the lights on, the window was wet black now like a puddle. Eamon and Mad Hugo were taking the hand out of Fluff in the corner. Walker was in for a while. There were a lot more people in the room than there were chairs for. The smoke drifted past the two lamps on the wall and up to the ceiling and he wondered if it was warmer up there and the voices were louder up there. Where do voices go? he said to Nuala and she banged her head with the palm of her hand at him. Harkin's da was pouring a can of stout into a glass on the arm of the sofa. Muck was hardening on the carpet with bits of grass stuck in the prints. The men's shoes were steaming which made him want to laugh. You see their shoes, he said to Nuala. She elbowed him and gave him that stare which meant listen to me with my hair hanging over my face. His Da was standing in front of the fireplace with his elbow on the mantelpiece between the clock that never worked and the fiddleplayer in the cage.

– Have a bet on it then? Put your money where your what-ever you call it is. There was about six of us and he was still kicking about. Aye, up near the reservoir. Didn't give in easy, I'll tell you that. Naw, on past that. Sure I had him by the leg. Aye, so I heard. He shouldn't have been out of the bloody house in the first place. That's what you get. Sure if you look at him the wrong way he goes up the stairs to huff. Aye. Hi Dandy, where's the wee woman the night? Aw aye. That's not what I heard. Who you kidding? Aye, Tony said it, some dogs alright. For fuck's sake, it was dripping off them when they came out. Aye, one of them was limping, I saw that my-self. Aye, the younger one. Aye, Walker'll be fucken sore if he's forced into it. I'd bet you my front teeth if I had any. Aye, but at least I didn't fucken sell mine, eh Larkey, and for what, eh for what?

74

The laughing.

Nuala was shaking her head in front of his face and her hair was flying around like she was falling down a hole. He took another taste of the whiskey. There must still be a thorn in his lip. Eamon helped him wash his face when they got back to the house. They walked home together through the streets only he couldn't remember all of it. There was nothing between Baldrick Hill and Florence Street. Nuala put her face right up to his ear and he saw the skull lying in the fire covered with pine needles the way her hair danced across the cuts on his face. She was saying she was there as well, hiding in the trees, and she saw the dogs go in and they came out again and nothing happened and they tore the roof off the hut and it was empty and nothing happened. Do you hear me Fergal? she was saying, there was nothing there. He heard her but he was thinking about the walk back with Eamon and whether it was an order from Walker or Eamon had put himself forward. That didn't matter anyway. An order is like a puddle in the street. The dog might drink from it but that doesn't mean it's thirsty. Eamon said that on Rosemount Avenue when they saw two mongrels bent over a puddle. One of them stopped first and then the other one ran back and started slurping beside it. Eamon stood watching them like it was important. The dogs ran on and the puddle settled and then the second one returned and had another drink, looking around like it thought it was being crafty. Eamon winked at him and talked about a dog they used to have called Sundance, a wee golden retriever. Fergal didn't remember it but Eamon insisted that he did and kept stopping in the streets and telling him. Fergal wondered that maybe he was making it up for a laugh but the way Eamon went on about it made it hard not to believe him. He said Sundance could do loads of tricks and you could never leave it alone in the house or it wouldn't look at you for days. Fergal didn't remember. Eamon went on about it the rest of the way down Rosemount and they never saw a single person. One day they let the dog out and it never came back he said, dabbing Fergal's face in the kitchen. It was probably running wild in the hills somewhere. Mad Hugo and a few others turned up with drink and sat down at the kitchen table. Mad Hugo made toast and gave Fergal a slice, but he didn't say anything. They were all talking about different things and the stories started up.

Skull Stick

All over the sloping street there are trails of green footprints. In and out of the shade where the dogs are lying, one-footed circuits of the cars parked in the sun, up on the pavement to people's doors, crisscrossing layers of dancing heel and toe in the cobbled gutter: Doctor is dancing. A car approaches from up the street and slows to a stop at a safe distance . . . a number of dogs drowsily lift their halloween heads. The driver fists his horn and, stepping out of the way, Doctor covers his face with his illuminated hands as if in pain. The car passes on across the wet tracks and carries the steps of the dance out through all the streets of London.

There you have an old black man dancing in the street in a woman's pink bathgown. On a summer's morning with a troupe of decorated dogs panting and tinkling in the shade. Above his head he swings a magical stick, a carved brush pole, and the skulls on their strings dangle from it and bounce and clatter together. There's a new addition this morning of a fresh pigeon's head with blood-filled, gloating eyes. Next thing there is a howl like the uplifted rage of ten men. Doctor's tongue is red and black stripes . . . he drops his gown from his shoulders. His spine is a crocodile in pink and blue, his sagging gut skin is a miasma of colour and fingerprints dapple his wrinkled neck. A plastic spoon swings from his old man's coloured-in cock. Wielding his stick, Doctor howls

79

again. An aeroplane is passing invisibly under the blue sky . . .
a woman looks out of an upper window, rubbing her eyes
between the shreds of curtains, and smiles.

Did he wake ye up as well, the mad bastard—that is Tally
now, the next thing, sitting down beside you on the sun-
warmed step in a pair of tartan boxer shorts and white t-shirt.
He relights the butt of a joint and offers it, but it's too early.
Fuck away off ya mad fucken jungleman, he shouts and he is
up off the step suddenly on the brink of something. Fuck
away off d'ye hear me with yer fucken dancing or I'm—Doctor howls and a sprayed mongrel looks skyward and echoes
the call. I mean it, says Tally as he sits again, he's doing my
fucken head in, I mean it, I'm going to lose it on him, I'm
telling you. A Belfast man is Tally, not allowed back they say.
The remnants of a burnt-off tattoo on his arm like the skin has
bubbled and overflowed the harp and the snake and permanent black teardrop under his right eye. His feet are delicate
and white and hairless. He says: I'm gonna lose it on him one
morning with that fucken stick. Tally; the correct outcome,
equilibrium, the reckoning, it all adding up and being how it
should be. So what's the crack with ye anyway Paul? Ye set-
tling in? It's not like home is it?

Doctor is displaying his highlighted arse to the half-risen sun.
Tally is talking about this teacher from years back who locked
himself in the classroom and set the building on fire. He drags
for the last time on the butt: So what ye up to the day then Paul?
Ye anything on? Doctor straightens and twists his neck to listen up and down the street to where it bends out of sight into
the sun haze. It's a fucken van to take you away ya mad cunt,
no more dancing for you cowboy, Tally laughs. Doctor starts
to come nearer like a painted naked man arriving out of the

sea. One more fucken step and it'll be your own fucken head on that stick, d'ye hear me? I'm not fucken joking ye wog man, I warned ye before remember—remember that fucken one eh, ya mad fucken headcase. Shouting, Tally is up on his small bare feet and there is a sealed sleeping eye at the back of each knee. Doctor raises his hand to quieten the din of the outraged multitude who follow him. Then he opens his mouth wide as though something is going to jump out. Tally flicks the butt straight at him and runs into the street . . . he bangs his fist on a car bonnet, banging and screaming: Y'see I can fucken do it as well, y'see, ye think yer mad do ye, ye think yer mad, I can fucken do it as well, I can fucken do it as well, ye listening, ye listening . . .

The birds tilt in flattened swarms around the back garden. In the windows opposite, there are glimpses of people moving around and making plans for the day. All over the city the join-the-dot crowds are mixing and re-forming and searching for the one more to complete the final picture and you are on your back on the bed without a dream in the blazing arena of the day. Tally wants to go swimming again; he said he would loan you his shorts as though he had no memory of the last time—You climbed out of the water for a dive and the whistle blasts ricocheted from wall to wall and Tally charged at the lifeguard who was trying to throw you out for obscenity in your see-through shorts. Afterwards Tally bought a bottle of cider. They sat by a canal and Tally talked to him about London like it was a dangerous animal which needed care and sacrifice. Later on they went to a pub and Tally paid and they played darts for a laugh and got into a competition with two English fellas who were living in a squat with a gay prostitute from Banbridge. Tally was supposed to wait outside on the street while he had a slash but there was no sign. When the pub was locked up he was still standing there. The road in both directions had the look of the track left behind after something terrifying had passed. And might be back. Two girls went past laughing and one reappeared to ask for a cigarette, and her fingertips were warm. Even then, he was incapable of asking where he was. There was nothing else to do but start walking. He walked the streets until it was light and nothing seemed to matter anymore.

The birds drop like a pile of bricks on the clothesline and swarm up again into the trees when Elaine the American girl steps into the garden to hang up her washing. The line hangs between the rusted swing and a pipe which runs up the side of the house to his open window and stops. She is a friend of Aisling, Eoin's girlfriend, and no one can establish how long she's planning to stay. Her red hair is straight and loose and she takes awkward steps in the dusty overgrown grass. She hasn't been out of bed long. When she reaches for a peg, her shirt slips up over the frail kite of her hips. Her skinniness is usually cloaked in a smog of twilight perfumes she will not have chosen yet. She is looking up now in the direction of his window, squinting or smiling liberally; she has either noticed his presence or she is anticipating the sun on the verge of making it over the rooftops.

You know I see you there, Paul, she says, shielding her eyes. I always know when somebody is watching me. It's a skill I have. She looks away from his window, at the matted garden and the houses and the empty unperfumed miles of blue above her. Then she lifts her face cheekily to him and says: Come down and talk to me, Paul. Please, Paul. She uses his name too much. Returning to her clothes, rearranging the pegs, she is trying to convince the world that she is never denied. The birds drift and reel and soar. Next thing she sits on the swing, which has a rotten length of wood for a seat between the rusted chains, and swipes with her bony legs in the trampled grass: So are you going to tell me where you've been hiding and why you're ignoring us? Are you trying to look mysterious and deep? She laughs and sweeps the hair from her face. Eoin said to me you're depressed. Is he right? She has this habit of asking questions which she likes to think are frank and straightforward. The first time they met was in Eoin's room watching a film when she slipped into the corner beside him and said, You and me are alike I think, we're both outsiders aren't we? She attempted to lay her head and her mournful fragrances on his shoulder but he found an excuse to move away.

You Irish are all mad, she decides to be controversial now and pushes herself back on the swing. All you ever do is talk about having a good time but none of you ever manage to do it. Or admit to it. Am I right? Her pale hands are gripping the cobwebbed chains in the bright sunlight. What do you do up in that bedsit all the time anyway, Paul? You'll never change anything that way. It merely carries on without you. She has her eyes closed as she swings. Hello world, she shouts, pretending she has a rampant appetite for all of it. Then she is hanging in mid-air, her eyes turned up towards you, strangely melancholy, her mouth open, and she lands firmly in the grass behind her washing. We're going to the park soon and you're coming with us Paul. Aren't you? She has her hands on her hips under her shirt, showing some of her narrow, mottled stomach. You are, Paul. Aren't I right?

Under the sun, now at its height over London, he is one of the shambolic crowd on the grass bank down to the canal: on the other side, a smoking violet marsh to a trio of scaffolded towerblocks against the jammed horizon. Jim and Manus are on the guitar and Badger is singing; Louise is making dreary noises on a harmonica; Macker and Gráinne, side by side on their backs, are talking intently and counting on their fingers; Miller; Joanne and Lisa; Eoin is there rolling a joint as always while Aisling is sitting with another group, most of whom are strangers; Tip who is painting his toenails and Joe who is telling a story about India. Elaine, using her pointed white knees, writes without shame in her diary in the midst of everyone. The drink is beer and warm vodka. Eoin wants to know about Doctor, what Tally was saying, if anything happened. Watch your back with him, Paul, he warns. He'll clean you out first chance he gets. He fucken broke into our room one time and nobody did a thing about it. Like we weren't allowed to talk about it or something because we all know the same streets. He licks the paper and gazes towards the canal where a dilapidated swan has come into view. Elaine slides in nearer, clutching her diary and her pen in her mouth: Do you want to know what I've been writing about? I heard it from Aisling. About this man who disappeared from your house. He was only here a few weeks like you. Nobody realised he had vanished until his sister arrived from Ireland. She waited in his bedsit for days but he didn't show up. Then she went back. She was getting married. That's all they knew. Eoin's got some of his books. Sci-Fi. And they've never heard of him again. She smiles complicitly and sucks on her pen: It's fascinating don't you think? The sun is a bright grave behind her head.

The towerblocks stand like the three legs of a gigantic table in progress where the resurrection book will be opened and everyone will hear their name and the tally figured out. A one-eyed swan zips and unzips the body-bag water to the sound of Manus strumming a guitar. Eoin has a lot of them listening to a story about his last trip on the bus back from Belfast with two men in front who were heading off to join the

Foreign Legion. He has long pale hair he keeps replacing behind his ears. The sun has its own tale of escape and failure as
Aisling drunkenly puts her freckled arm around you and
kisses your neck. You're always so calm, she says. Tell her it's
all dead, the sun and kissing, tell her the sun is as cold as the
ferry windows and the vodka is the taste of the rain under the
bus wheels taking you away, tell her the stories are useless
and savage and the words for it all floating loose and drifting
like disfigured swans slamming their brains out against the
hardened water; Aisling in her vest without a bra who thinks
nothing of leaving Eoin in the night to sneak into your room
with a joint. Your head is lowered against hers and you can
see down inside her vest to the sweat in her spread cleavage
. . . Next thing Elaine has her scrawny arms around both of
you and saying how good she feels and what a wonderful day
it is. Eoin is looking at you . . . he winks and wants to know
what happened in the dole then.

It was just that he stayed too long. He went over to the chairs
and sat down instead of leaving straight away like you're
supposed to. For no reason that was clear to him, he sat there
for an hour and watched the ones coming in off the drained
summer streets and felt both sickened and comforted by the
intricate turmoil of so many lives. A girl was sleeping beside
him on one of the plastic chairs. With twists of coloured string
in her black hair. He counted twenty rings in the ear he could
see. On the floor the sun slowly clarified the handiwork of the
metal window grille. Eventually, two cops came into the hall
behind the hefty figure of a tramp with a filthy grey beard and
a battered overstuffed bag . . . the tramp pointed tri-
umphantly at the sleeping girl. Each of the cops in turn tried
to waken her; they spoke to her in loud and gentle voices,
nudged her shoulder, clapped their hands and tapped her

sandalled feet with their polished boots. After some delibera-
tion, one of the cops retreated into a corner and seemed to
blush as he turned on his radio. By this time, a small crowd
had gathered and were watching with amusement. Overcome by an urge to sort the matter out for himself, the tramp
made a grab for the girl's hair but the second cop was quick to
step in the way . . . the crowd booed the old tramp who was
shouting about angles or handles. He was ordered to stand
back. It was at this point that the girl jumped out of her chair
with a knife in her hand—a blade with a white padded handle like a pincushion. She screamed at the crowd to stand
back which they all did without hesitation, some making for
the door, laughing and pushing each other. One of the cops
began to approach the girl, his hands out in front of him as
though it would soothe her, his nostrils flared. The girl lowered her head like she was about to run at him. Perhaps she
saw the tramp behind him finally lose his patience and drop
his bag, for when he pushed the cop out of the way and stood
in front of her with his arms outspread like he was the wind,
she was ready for him and pushed the knife deep into him
through the overcoat. The tramp turned his eyes towards the
ceiling and roared in fury. As he went down on his knees, his
hands clutching his beard, she called him a liar and a fake and
a spoof. Her voice was Irish, northern, farmstock, dark bare
hills and cratered roads. The crowd looked confused and
sceptical because there was no stain of blood; some stood
aside, expecting her to make a run for the door but she
seemed enchanted by the sight of the old man's suffering. Reluctantly, with their heads lowered and their cheeks sucked
in, the two cops started to move towards her.

The stars always make you want to remember something: say
that to her. The moon is behind a tree trying out different

disguises. A mohican punk with the gestures of a robot is pursuing a wailing girl around the garden . . . suddenly she turns, brandishing a flower and the robot tips over on his back with his legs in the air . . . the girl then transforms into a vampire and flings herself on the robot's throat. Candle flames are wriggling like everything you have forgotten in old whiskey bottles on the other empty tables—all this behind Elaine's pinched face across a picnic table in a pub garden. She will not be diverted from the course of her questioning now that she has you alone under the stars. She wants an explanation for dropping out of university and coming to London. What do you think you're going to find here that you didn't have in Belfast, she asks and lights a cigarette and waits. Have you come just to waste away like the rest of them? That's no achievement. Anyone could do that. Her long thin chin and a small nose and limp red hair—there's a scantness in everything she does, in the way she holds a cigarette or touches her hair or frowns or glances at the stars, in her scratchy voice and skeletal presence like nothing can feed her or please her under the nervous grin and the questions and the faked excitement.

During the band's first set, she seized his hand and dragged him out to dance in such a way that he had no choice. Her eyes shut, she squirmed to the music like a twig wedged in the gutter on a windy street. Badger was doing the Par Avion song about leaving this girl behind among the barricades and the smoke and the weeping women. Eoin and Aisling were kissing in the middle of the floor after their argument in the park, the day congealing into pinks and greens like the one poisoned eye of a demented swan. The bar was crowded and fervent and a humid fog of sweat and perfume stretched from the stage to the open front door where another group of punks were letting on they were bouncers.

On his way back from the toilet, a girl tried to talk to him; she wanted to know what he was doing there. Her eyelids moved like they were her lips. She stepped in front of him each time he tried to get by her. Unable to convince her that he didn't know who she was, he went out into the garden where he could always say he was feeling sick if he was accused of the blasphemy of not joining in. You always look so sad, was the first thing Elaine said when she found him again. She stood looking down at him, her arms folded, convicting him of sorrow. She asked if she could sit down. That was the moment to put a stop to it before she could speak and draw him into the starved constellations that her pity is. She sat down anyway without waiting for an answer, probably flattering herself for her audacity. There was a round of applause and shouting from inside as the band finished their set.

Thin and frugal against her will, Elaine smokes her cigarette and flagrantly tries to outdo his silence. They are the only ones in the garden now. The moon has selected a funereal pink for its last number of the evening. There is a very particular item that she wants to know about, proof of her insight and communion. Her other hand lies across the table, the tip of each unpainted finger pressed firmly into the wood as though she is afraid of falling. I dropped out of university as well you know, she says then. I've first-hand knowledge of how lonely it feels. And then leaving everyone you know for a strange city. But I realised the world didn't care, Paul. No one was watching or noticed my anger. No one hears you crying, Paul, she says and places the butt upright on the table. Tell her . . .

. . . there's nothing to go back for, nothing to remember, not even the loneliness, not even the words for it and you've no way of saying that and that's the whole point, and that's why there's all those unused moons and the sprinkled stars of

88

boredom and the silence and stoned days-out in a luminous park, tell that to her. She pulls her jacket around her tighter and sighs . . . and says, Feel my hands. London is always so cold. Her knuckles under your hand are like four nauseating hills in the dust and flatness at the end of the world. From the bar there is another bout of shouting and Badger's comes back to the mic: Alright there youse crowd of drunken eejits, youse ready for more? This next one's about this fella we went to school with an'all and he turned out to be a grass. So say nothing and watch the shadows at your back.

They are walking home together—that's what is happening, that's the next thing, there's always a next thing, and it's only the pain that connects them. They are walking through the overused streets and her arm is slight and cold and twisted in his. Beneath an unsteady light she stops to tie back her hair, without a break in her talk. Her shrill voice echoes along the street ahead of them, invading the darkest lairs of silence and forgotten corners and scattering the pigeons from an old window. The cars touch and touch and touch. I'm so stoned, she says with a girlish skip like she did in the garden earlier, are you? Why are you so quiet? You make it feel like it would shame you to say a single word. They pass people sitting on the ground outside a kebab shop, eating and staring. A couple holding each other tightly in a doorway. A bicycle that she says looks like it has melted around the lamp-post. Houses and shops and indeterminate places that are badly lit altars to direction and movement. I often notice how short the streets are here, she sighs and squeezes your arm, happy with herself for having found something interesting to say. There's nothing long and broad and straight to the horizon. Why do you think that is, Paul?

Doctor's dried footprints are scattered across the street like leaves in the darkness and under the lights there are paw-marks and strange scuffs of paint which might even have been birds, or maybe worse. Elaine is laughing now under the young tree but she doesn't want to explain. You would probably take it the wrong way, she says blithely, as though she wants him to admit that she can see through the disorder of his mind. Just then he notices that most of the lights are on in the house; otherwise he would have told her once and for all that they had absolutely nothing in common, no matter how many words for it she used or how many ways she tried to drum up her vision of them as melancholy outcasts whose paths have fatefully crossed.

The key won't turn in the door, that's the next thing. Through the letterbox he can see the greasy finger-stained globe of the banister, a bare bulb at the end of an unravelling wire, the soft wax and woodchip walls, the dog-eared carpet tiles and half-open door into Tally's room with a poster of an IRA funeral pinned to it . . . Try the doorbell, Elaine says as she does it herself and pushes it again as though it was more important for her to be let inside than anything that might conceivably have happened. What, for example? she drawls. Murder? You've been watching too much television. Is that what you do with all the time in your room?

The door has two oblong stained-glass panes above the letterbox with its knocker that is too stiff and rusting and hangs stuck in a gesture of alarm or mockery. Then there are voices from inside. Through the letterbox the hall is bright and empty for a few seconds before a pair of split-new white trainers appears on the landing and begins to descend the stairs two at a time, jumping the last stretch and running into Tally's room. Close behind, comes a pair of battered suede boots and camouflaged trousers, more slowly than the first, even lingering in the hall before backing away towards

Tally's door. What's happening, Paul? Is somebody there? Elaine is jumping up and down to keep warm . . . There on the bottom stair now is a pair of polished ox-blood DMs with black laces and pressed jeans and that is Tally without question, in defiance, in temptation, waiting, daring, standing on the rope of your gaze. What's wrong, Paul? What's there? Elaine cries out, her arms raised like the door knocker, in the name of safety or loss, as you pull yourself free from the sight of Tally. She puts her arms around you. Over her shoulder you can see Doctor's tracks like the crazed spoor of . . . the lock is flicked open behind you, a bout of laughter and the bedroom door slams shut.

You can't walk away, no matter how much you want to. You can't walk away like you would do if you were alone. A shivering dry-lipped American pushes you towards a confrontation with Tally who caught you red-handed as a witness. On the way up the stairs, all the bedsit doors have been kicked in. The door of Eoin's room is lying across his bed. Elaine goes in to check on her stuff and comes out again, smiling, and then follows you to the top of the house. Jammed into the open window the mattress is a monstrous letter, the drawers are ransacked, a tap is running full-blast and pages of books cover the floor. The disorder is familiar in some way; Elaine frowns at the very idea of that and shakes her narrow head. Shall I call the police? she says, holding out her arms. Don't touch anything, Paul. Evidence, she whispers.

He pulls her shirt out of her jeans. Her skin seems to tense and ebb away under his hand and makes him think of a stain drying. Under the coarse lace, her stingy breasts, unclutchable, the cold miniature nipples: Paul, stop, what are you doing? she gasps . . . but he goes for her crutch, trying to get his hand down inside her trousers. Elaine manages to wriggle free and runs to the window with the mattress stuck in it, her face burning: Not now Paul, not here, we can't, please. As she is talking, one of her hands strokes the edge of the mattress.

Downstairs then, they hear voices. The image of the murky red boots on the stairs comes back to him and a fight in the swimming pool in transparent togs and the black teardrop under Tally's eye. Had he been waiting all day to go swimming? Tally was in the room enough to know there was nothing worth stealing. It was some other force driving him, an anger he carried over from the Belfast streets, housing estates at the foot of scalped, discoloured hills, the constant ache in the eyes and the ash from a smoke-bitter wind which gathers under the tongue no song or prayer or curse can ever dislodge.

Wankers, he hears called up from the hall. A Belfast voice . . . The front door bangs shut and with a shiver he listens to them singing in the street like it is his own name they are sending up to heaven. Elaine is pulling at the mattress: Ignore them, she says. What good are they to anybody? That one, Tally, he's in big trouble already from what I hear. He was thrown out of Ireland wasn't he?

In this room they are all gathered to debate the course of action. The blond Englishman from the bedsit downstairs squats in the doorway, in shorts and a leather waistcoat. On the bed where Elaine cried herself to sleep, Aisling sits and twists the coils of rings on her fingers. Eoin has the trampled manic air of glut and despondency after the day out but Aisling might have just stepped out of her room after a day on her own. He's a fucken madman, Eoin strides about in the room and whispers out of respect for the sleeper. Does he think we're all going to pretend we don't know who it was? I've had enough, I'm not afraid of him. Then he begins for the second time to record on his fingers the extent of the theft from his room. I'm having déjà vu, the blond man giggles. Tranquil and sorrowful, Aisling gets to her feet, crosses the room and takes a cigarette from Eoin's pocket . . . she returns to the bed where she takes a drag on the unlit cigarette. A light goes on in a house across the dark froth of the garden where the swing stands in the hyped yellow light from the kitchen like a walking frame for a crippled giant.

We owe that fucker nothing, Eoin implores, standing above you with wrecked eyes and a long sagging face. Did you see anything, Paul? He reels away from your silence, spinning in a circle: It was fucken Tally. We all know it was. We fucken do. It was him. I'm calling the police, he announces in an anguished voice, and there are tears in his eyes he lets his hair hang forward to hide.

You're worse than any cop, Aisling says with a vacant face, and as she is leaving the room she lays her pitying hand on your head. A few seconds later, the blond man leaves without a word. Elaine sleeps like a twig under the water of the blankets. He won't touch you, Eoin slides down the wall to sit opposite. Gripping his kneecaps, he tries to reassure you: You fucken owe him nothing, Paul. Why are you protecting him? He's a bastard and it doesn't matter a fuck where he comes from. Fuck all that loyalty and say nothing stuff, Paul.

A woman in a dressing gown stands with a wine glass in her hand at a window across the garden. Away in the background there's singing. Out there in the London night there's the steps of a dance drying under a blazing moon and skulls rattling and bouncing on a stick and carnival dogs chewing their tinsel bandages. Paul, just tell me, Eoin moans from behind his wet fingers. Did you see him? Don't let him away with it. Just tell me. Give me one word. One word. His eyes running with tears, he beseeches you. And all you can think about is another night when . . .

93

. . . a night outside a pub when Tally left you stranded on the street and two girls went by with their laughter and one came back with warm fingers in search of a cigarette and you didn't know where you were or the way home or anywhere else and you couldn't ask you were that afraid or finally relieved, so there was nothing left to do but walk and walk the darkened streets until the light and the sudden morning crowds and even then you sat in a park still not asking the way near some old water and a train track trying to persuade yourself that the choice was a bad trick and you had to do it and ask or else—although there was no reason that day pale as a candle flame and futile and it was so possible not to bother and give in to the temptation to stay out there on the streets in the smirking dusk and walk in silence and filth and never ask the way back of anyone in those crowds rushing and streaming home again who knew there was no reason and pitied nothing neither the dark or the light or that there could be no reason ever again . . .

Dans La Rue

She opens her eyes and the tears leak in. Back inside her head, a cold trickling behind her eyeball. She blinks and blinks until she can see the house. These are not tears. Rain is filling up her eyes, a soft mizzle on her retina. She lies with her eyes open to the rain in the night. There is a boy in the next street with a big head, they say has water on the brain. Your mother wore a flared pink dress and a green wig and when she rubbed her eyes and cried the tears spouted out and sprinkled the stage. Rain washes away nothing.

This is not a bed.
   This is not a pillow.
   These are not tears.

The girl blinks and sees that the door of the house is open and the mizzle swirling like insects in the light from the hall. The darker shape on the kitchen door at the end of the hall is a hole where her mother put her foot through. The girl looks up at a plant like the head of a long-haired prisoner in the window of the room where her mother never sleeps. A flight of stairs in the brightness should not be seen from the street at night.

There are no walls here. No ceiling.
   The breeze is not coming through an opened window.
   The rain neither.

There is no chance this is a bedroom.

Late one night, a woman comes along the street and stops beside a girl lying on a sofa. The woman sits and smooths aside the damp fringe of hair on the girl's forehead. The woman's own hair is hidden under a scarf, although she is not old. She has thin nostrils and her fingertips are cold like tears but not her small eyes. Her eyes are dark and small and stare at the ground while her hand strokes the girl's head. The look of worry for someone and the look of hurt are the same. On a sofa in the street for a woman and a girl. Under the oldness of the sky.

Poor dote, the woman whispered and blessed herself.

There is no hope the sky is old. Gently, the woman squeezes your shoulder and goes then in her flat shoes and scarf. Down the street and over the zebra crossing and along the edge of the wasteground. You wriggle your toes in your mother's shoes and pull the coat up around your chin. A man's coat with the smell of under the bed. Like you were a puddle he laid the coat across you for a lady to step on. On her way to the ball. Under the collar there is a leather loop for the hook of a door you can put your tongue through. Three boys run past and jump together over a puddle in the street with their hands in their pockets. If a fire is lit in the wasteground, a crowd will lay their eyes on an open house and the furniture out on the street and get big ideas about tall and lurching flames. A strange man keeps a battered matchbox in his pocket half-filled with sand.

The world is heavier when it's wet.

Time góes slower.

There were more farms before the Industrial Revolution.

Il pleut n'est-ce pas?

98

White sheets were pinned over the classroom windows. The women gathered in front of the mirror, laughing, singing, wiping off their make-up. Mrs Lynch, who taught geography, was wearing a black suit and tie and her hair was flattened down with shoe polish. The chairs were upside down on the tables. Mr Gallagher came in the door without knocking and the women screamed and threw things at him until he left. A brush hit the wall and made a rip in the poster of a city with the French words for a house, a street, a car, a tree, a bus, a shop and an aeroplane and clouds and birds in the sky.

I've been wanting to do that for years, your mother said laughing and filled the women's cups with red wine.

You were walking between the tables in your mother's high heels.

What's wrong with you? you heard.

Your mother was sitting on the floor, hiding her face behind the wig.

What's the matter with you?

Your mother tried tearing the wig with her hands but it was too strong. She threw the wig on the floor where it looked like a flattened cloud of green smoke.

I'm sick of this, she was saying. Tears were coming out of one eye and turning the colour of milk on their way down her face. I'm sick of this. Sick to the bloody teeth of everything.

Les meubles sont dans la rue.

Fires leave stains on the wasteground like shadows. Of invisible things hovering above your head. The sofa leaves six long scratch lines from the door to the street and the TV wheels another four. The chair another four. The coffee table is on its back with the legs in the air like an insect. The mattress clings to a rectangle of concrete. The shadows of three boys cross the surface of a puddle. But the houses vanish if you close your eyes. The sky leaves no trace when you close your eyes. The street disappears.

Damp will rust the mattress springs.
   Rust is a residue of decomposing metal.
   Rust makes more noise.

The girl counts seventeen steps from the sofa to the front door. Seventeen times she drags one heel after another across the tarmac and concrete and through the puddles. Her night-dress is a long t-shirt from America with a picture on it of Charlie Chaplin in his big shoes and bowler hat and swinging his cane. The banisters on the stairs are chipped and scratched by the furniture like a prisoner has been locked up in the house, counting the sunrises for centuries. In the light of the hall she takes her feet out of the shoes and listens.

She listens. To the stairs, the light bulb, the carpet, the wall-paper, to her room up above, to a siren far off, her own breathing, the damp drying in her hair, snoring in the front room, the glass in the kitchen door, the mizzle. She lifts one foot and places it down again farther along the hall. Her foot makes a noise like someone sitting down on a sofa. Holding her breath, she reaches the door of the front room and sees her mother lying in the middle of the floor, next to the cabinet. The woman she sees on the floor has her hands wrapped around her head as people do when they are afraid of being blown to pieces. The woman's skirt is caught up around her hips, showing her pale blue knickers which are crooked and wet. Her blouse is torn under the arm. The glass door of the cabinet is smashed and the pieces sprinkled all over the car-pet and a bottle stands upright in the pieces like it has been made and born from them. A cat appears at the kitchen door and looks at the both of them sulkily, rubs itself against the wall and saunters out. Cats make less noise than furniture.

A drunk woman snores on the floor of a house.

A man goes off to America.

A cat sneaks in through an open door.

Broken glass stops making any noise after a while.

Through the window the girl watches a fight around the furniture in the street. One boy is swinging a chain at three other boys and a girl. He dances and dodges the stones coming at him but he knows there's no strength in their throws, no determination, so he is smiling and laughing at them as he whips the air and the ground with the chain. The boy is sitting on the sofa with his legs crossed under him when the girl comes out of the house again, trailing her feet in her mother's high heels.

– I saved your sofa, he says as she sits and drapes herself in the strange man's jacket.

– No one asked you to.

– There's a lorry burning down the road, he says, squinting, as though he is trying to remember if he is telling the truth. And a woman up here who can't get to sleep with the noise of the sofa and chairs.

– Shout something, the girl tells him.

The boy has fat dark lips and big ears. He always has the look of being about to sneeze. He is wearing trousers torn off at the knees. In the nights when he comes to sit with her, he pushes a wheelbarrow.

– Shout something.

– Like what?

– Jist shout something.

He takes a deep breath. Tomorrow, he shouts out. He looks at her then.

– Did you hear an echo?

– Tomorrow, he shouts again and seems to listen.

He shakes his head. Can you?

– I can, the girl tells him.

– You're lying.

– Only if I'm saying something I am sure is not true, she says. At least I have a mother.

What's the French for wheelbarrow? the boy wants to know, turning to face her on the sofa, touching her with his scabbed knee. He looks at her with his mouth open as though she might put the answer on his tongue. Like a big black wreath, there is a tyre lying in the wheelbarrow. He said that he throws them like hoops at the chimneys.

Two men appear in front of them. One of them is tall with a bald head and glasses and a smirk on his lips.

The sea turns the ground to sand.

And riots.

One of the men has his hand wrapped in a bandage. His double chins need a shave. Two men stare at a girl and a boy on a sofa in the street.

– Knock knock, says the fat one, tapping his head with his injured hand.

– Who's there? says Smiler and taps your shoe with the toe of his own and winks an eye with long lashes at you.

– *Qui est là?*

He shakes his head and sighs with disappointment. She's not doing it right, he complains to the Smiler, who takes off his glasses and pretends to look shocked and disbelieving.

– My mother's sleeping, you say.

– Do you want me to go and check on her? asks the injured one.

– She's sleeping.

– She's some woman. Dragging that furniture about.

– And this one, the Smiler says about the boy, is he annoying you?

The boy is hiding his face behind his hands.

– He's sleeping, you tell them.

– Great shoes, says the fat one. You'll be up on the stage soon like your mother.

The two men turn to watch someone else running bent at the waist along the street and straight through the puddle.

A boy sleeps behind his hands. Behind you on the floor of the house your mother sleeps with her hands over her head like she is being searched. Charlie Chaplin spreads his handkerchief across his hat and lays down on it. Watching a film with her, when the tramp's cabin was balanced on the edge of a cliff and she got up to make some tea and she started to push the furniture from one wall to the other like the house was going to tip over the edge. At night you carried a basin of boiling water up the stairs, trying not to spill any. From the stairs you could see her in the bedroom, in a chair with her head between her knees, under a towel, wheezing, sucking in the moisture. The steam floated around her and rose up and stuck to the mirror over her head. In her high heel shoes you went over on your ankle and let the basin drop and the water scalded her leg. She dragged you down the stairs by the hair and made you watch as she threw the shoes out into the dark in the wasteground . . .

Heat turns the sand into mirrors.

A matchbox of sand is a small grave.

The boy stands up and stamps his feet. He pulls up his hood, puts his hands in his pockets and looks down the street like it is nowhere he knows.

. . . You waited all night, watching the dark deepen and shiver and crumble like a mirror dying, but the shoes were gone from the puddles and firemarks and blackened grass in the morning. A boy was going along the street and he stopped to look at you. You saw the shoes in his wheelbarrow.

The street is quiet. *La rue est tranquille*. A girl like herself goes to school and grows into a woman. And a teacher of French. And a drunk deafened by the furniture. Furniture roars and taunts her when she shuts her eyes. The boy's face is the same colour of the sky inside his hood. He is whistling to himself, through his teeth. The puddles shake because the rain is getting heavier. Your mother brought you pink bath salts from Paris which made a grit in the bottom of the bath. The salts were kept on the window ledge in a thick glass bottle with a ribbon. One night she decided to wash the windows and poured the salts into a bucket of warm water and carried a stool outside to stand on. You watched her do one window and start on the second and then walk away up the street with the cloth in her hand as though she saw somebody there she wanted to give it to.

In the middle of the street, a bin has been turned upside down with the number 14 in red paint on it. Number 14 is the Duffy's. James Duffy has a swollen head and they say he has water on the brain. Now furniture keeps your mother awake and the sky above the houses and the streets will never ever be old.

You can fall asleep if you look in a mirror too long.

Or stare at a house.

– Can I go with you this time? she says to the boy.

He picks up the handles of the wheelbarrow.

– What about your mother? he says angrily. And all this furniture? It'll be swiped.

– I could sit in the front and you could wheel me, the girl says, standing up in her mother's shoes. She puts her arms into the strange man's jacket.

– Where is it we're going? she asks him, buttoning the jacket over the picture of Charlie Chaplin.

He doesn't answer.

– Where?

– Jist around the streets, he says like it is a duty. He lifts the tyre out of the wheelbarrow and sends it rolling down the street out of sight into the darkness.

– You're not allowed to annoy me, he says then. No more French.

Through the rain a boy with his hood up pushes a girl in a wheelbarrow. Across the wasteground to other streets sheltered by the same night. A dog follows them for a time. The girl lets her legs hang over the rusty rim of the wheelbarrow so that sometimes the heels of her mother's shoes scratch the ground or break through a puddle or knock a stone out of the way. The fat wheelbarrow wheel squeaks and it stiffens if directed to the right. The boy always knows where he is going, even at crossroads or where a street stops in the middle of nowhere. People look at them and there are some who don't. The girl lies back in the wheelbarrow and holds her eyes open to the rain. In this city her mother is sleeping on the floor of an emptied house and any stranger can walk in and see her stained knickers. In another city in America, there is a man who is her father. Rain washes away nothing. These are not tears. The boy is whistling again, through his teeth. The wheel leaves the concrete behind and bounces and hisses through the grasses and muck.

Portraiture

I am sitting with Aoife in a café in the centre of town. Every Sunday morning we come here for our breakfast. I will always have the bacon, chips and peas but Aoife is not so predictable; this morning, she ordered a glass of milk and scrambled eggs. She has finished eating now and her newspaper is spread out across the table. Her hands are hidden inside the sleeves of one of my shirts: for some reason, Aoife likes to wear my clothes after a night out on the town. As she reads, her head moves discreetly in time to a song on the radio behind the counter. I find it impossible to read in public places—or anywhere I am not alone. Aoife will tell me about anything interesting. She might read it aloud to me but usually she puts it into her own words. She presses her lips together when she reads. I can see she is bored when her tongue appears and touches the rough skin at the corners of her mouth. There have been mornings she has read for nearly an hour without speaking or even glancing over at me. This morning she looks up at me suddenly as if she has just remembered something crucial. I look back at her and wait for an explanation, but she shakes her head and impatiently pulls the shirtsleeves away from her hands. She begins to tear a neat line down the page of the newspaper; about half way down, she loses patience and roughly rips the page apart. People look over at us. She holds out the strip of paper towards me. Her brown eyes seem amused and astonished at the same time. She is breathing through her nose. I try to refuse the scrap in her hand—she knows I can't read it in the café—but Aoife lays it calmly on the table in front of me, smooths it flat with her palm and turns her roused eyes away towards the window and the empty Sunday street.

– I was sick of the world. I was young but I already knew there was no relief. I wanted nothing from any of them. 'What is the matter with you? Why are you so angry?' they asked and never listened to the answer. I walked the streets and sneered. They tried to pity me. Then some of the more banal began to believe that it was me who pitied them. So they taught themselves to loathe me. I slept on the streets and grew sick. I was young but the doctors still wouldn't leave me alone. I was at the point of suicide when I met her.

– How did you meet her?
– No questions. You agreed.
– Just tell me how you met her.

I wait in silence until she gives up. Aoife lies naked on the bed across the room, her arms by her side and her legs crossed at the ankles. Two tall multicoloured candles are burning on the table near her head. A long cloud of yellow light floats above her body.

– Promise?
– Cross my heart, says Aoife and does it, grazing her breast with her finger.
– She was younger than me, this girl, I continue. Younger in many ways. There was a naturalness about her, a tormenting naturalness, in her slight body, the excess of fine hair on her arms and back. She always wore a scruffy summer dress and battered suede boots. Her knees were spoiled like a child's.

Wherever she went she attracted attention, but she could never understand why. She would stop to speak to strangers on the street, spend the entire day with them simply because she liked how they looked or something they said. Her hair was dark blonde, almost yellow around her temples. She could sit with a lonely man for hours in a pub and wonder why he turned hostile when she suddenly stood up to leave. She had no secrets. She listened to everyone, fascinated. I wanted her to myself. One night I persuaded her to leave the city with me. Call her Deirdre.

Aoife squeals with laughter and rolls over on to her front.

– Deirdre?

– You swore.

– I know. But Deirdre. Pick a different one. What was her real name?

– Does she have one?

Aoife laughs and turns on to her front. Sighing, she drops her face into the pillow and says something I don't hear. Her crossed feet rise up slowly and then she lets them fall heavily back on to the bed. She lifts her head out of the pillow.

– Please, no Deirdres. Whether it happened or not. That's not a Deirdre you're describing anyway. A Nuala or a Joanna. Or an Ann or Kate. Or a Fiona. Ruth even. Call her Ruth. I bet she had money. I bet she did. I'm right aren't I?

– This is your last chance, I tell her. Lie down again.

Aoife settles herself noisily again on her back. The candle flames sway and veer with her movement, throwing a huge shadow of her body on the wall. On the shelf beside the plant, I catch a glimpse of the rag of newspaper I had thrown away in the street. The light in the room slows and settles like a thick gold meniscus.

– She had a car anyway, I start again. We drove out of the city. I had nothing and she had little more than a sleeping bag.

We stole a tent from a campsite and drove on. There was a de-
crepit bit of shore where we stopped and found a cave she
was eager to explore – all leaking, thwarted grandeur. In some
dawdling town or other, I made her stop to buy a bottle: she
came out of the shop with three men at her side. It wouldn't
have surprised me if she had invited them along. We drove
on, through the dusk and into the night, with no idea where
we were going. I was drunk and seething, you see. I lay in the
back seat, interrogating her, shouting at her, laughing at her.
I don't remember why but we finally stopped by a broken
gate on some hillside. I climbed into the front and made her
drink some of the whiskey. She was quiet but I could be more
quiet. She sat with her knees up on the steering wheel. I relied
on the silence to frighten her. I had never touched her before,
you see. What's the matter? she said to me at last. Are you
bored with me already? I must have taken a second too long
to answer for Ruth dropped her knees and twisted the key in
the ignition.

– Much better, Aoife says in a teacherly voice. Now her
hands are joined under her breasts, pushing them upwards,
their shadow unsteady and obscenely big on the wall. Her
head is tilted back on the blue pillow. She has unlinked her
feet, spread her legs wide, the right knee turned towards the
wall. I want to ask her why she has stopped wearing the silver ring on her toe.

– I grabbed Ruth by the hand. She was crying, her head
bowed over the steering wheel. The headlights flared point-
lessly in the darkness. Nothing's ever happened to me worth
talking about, she said. I'm boring you. I risked everything
and agreed with her: I moved my hand along her arm to her
shoulder and under her hair. The skin on her neck was cold. I
told her to drink more. She sat back and put her knees up
against the steering wheel, trapping her printed frock under

her so that I could see the white bulked flesh of her thigh up to the hip and the band of her underwear. I ran my hand down the front of her dress in search of her breasts. Finish it, I said, giving her the whiskey again. She shook her head. I told her again to finish it. She swallowed what she could and held her breath to stop herself from vomiting. I poured what was left across her thigh: I was deranged by her, you see—if there had been a knife in the car I would have wanted to slash the seats.

What are you doing? she screamed. I held both her hands and pulled her towards me and started kissing her mouth. My tongue was burning: the drink made me sullen and crazy. She had thin hard lips that reminded me of worms. I sank back on the seat and laughed like an idiot. I laughed and slapped the dashboard. The headlights fizzled relentlessly, outside in the dark, in my eyes.

It's my fault, Ruth said when I quietened down. I'm listening, she said. I had hidden my face in my hands, you see. I'd do anything, she whispered and her hand touched my hair. Her eyes were grave and frightened when I looked at her. I couldn't breathe. I opened the car door and vomited in the grass: the long grass crushed and trapped by the car made me think of her spread legs. You see I wanted to be nothing in her eyes: I took out my cock and rubbed it between my hands. Sweat dripped into my eyes. Ruth was crying again. I wanted her in some way I was incapable of imagining. Grabbing her hand, I closed it around my cock—I could tell straight away that she had never done this before, which only increased my feeling of desolation. I was crying now too, and laughing. I wanted to see her looking at me with disgust. I was crying because I wanted to feel ashamed in front of her. I took a cigarette butt from the ashtray and started chewing it.

Over on the bed, I notice the movement of Aoife's hand which has covertly found its way to her right breast, the tightening and loosening of her knuckle, gently grasping and releasing the flesh. I ask myself whether she knows I can see her or not, whether she hopes I see her or if she would prefer the thrill of subterfuge.

Aoife waited for me outside the café while I paid. For nearly an hour after she had given me the newspaper article, we sat on in the café and invented characters and motives and scenes until I grew tired and annoyed with this new tendency of hers towards the fantastic and the frivolous. She kept an embarrassing distance behind me on the street: when two men with dogs appeared from a house, she started shouting and begging me to stop and not to leave her. I made a ball of the paper I was still holding in my hand and dropped it into the gutter. Her footsteps stopped and then I heard her running behind me.

– Police in Italy have launched a manhunt for a kidnapper who abducted the famous and respected artist Fausto Atelurba at gunpoint, she read the story aloud again, breathlessly, drove him to a hotel and forced him to paint a portrait of a beautiful young woman. We forgot about the hotel. Why a hotel? Was he ashamed of his own place? Maybe the beautiful young woman refused to have her portrait done in impecunious environs, with the rats sitting on the windowsill trying to make her laugh, and destroying her ambiguous smile? Maybe they didn't trust the imaginative power of the famous Fausto to overcome the soul-destroying poverty? Or they might have been tourists? Or art terrorists in for a flying visit? Aliens, they might have been aliens, trying to learn how to paint. Do you think he knew the beautiful young woman? Or did he kidnap her too? A new crime—drive-by portraiture. Serial portraiters. Pounce and Paint. A premeditated act of portraiture. Where are you going?

– I don't know, I said. For a walk. Anywhere.

– Are you annoyed with me? she laughed. She held my arm and kissed me. I want to show you something.

– Like what? I said, expecting another joke or pun from her. You're just going too far with this and I can't see why.

– So, instead, you're going to walk to nowhere and back again, Aoife said, trying to restrain a smile. I want to show you something.

– I didn't say anything about coming back again, I told her, smiling myself now.

Aoife put her arm around mine and pulled me along the street.

– You know, I'm happy today, she said, looking up and shaking her head with serene defiance under the sky.

– I wake up in the car, freezing and nauseous. Outside there's a low, morbid mist—nothing is visible below the knee. I feel exhausted. I walk blindly into the middle of what must be a field: I must have tripped and fallen down. In front of me, I can't tell how far, a black hump of a hill, streaked with brown: I only see it after I've fallen over. A silent bird, maybe a kestrel, hovers above the scarred slopes. I have this idea that the hill—the hill will subside and crumble under my feet like a mountain of coal or slack when I reach there. I am going towards this featureless mound with the last of my strength.

Her hair in long wet strands, panting, Ruth appears beside me. She has been for a swim she tells me, swinging a plastic bag of food. I point towards the hill. You see that black dump of a shitheap there, I say, but Ruth tells me I don't look well and that I should rest. She strokes my face: Take off your clothes, I tell her suddenly, grabbing her by the shoulders.

I beg her, ignoring her plea that she's cold. I am convinced

115

that only her naked body can distract me from the dark hill—
I don't know what's wrong with me, you see. I lift up her
frock above her waist and bury my face in her white underwear. The brittle pale hair spills out across her thighs: I suck
on the hair, pull at it with my teeth. Now she holds her dress
in one hand like a defeated flag. I look up the length of her
body, her white clean belly, the small, unsuccessful breasts,
her wet hair, her eyes closed—the sight of her shut eyes is like
a kick in the stomach, the breath leaves me. I pull her down
on the grass and she doesn't even flinch at the morning wet
against her skin. I strip her bare. The gross black bump in the
mist—Nothing grows there, I shout out.

Ruth is lying in the grass, as still as a corpse, her eyes closing: a kind of stinging pain rushes through my veins. I take
out my cock, work on myself but I am not aroused. I am raging for her and I am not aroused. I want her flesh between my
teeth, I want to devour her like an animal and all I feel is useless rage. I'm sorry, she says in the car when we're back on the
road. She is crying again, but silently. I am wrapped in the
sleeping bag to keep warm. The sun is everywhere, crowding
the fields, lying in ditches, waiting at crossroads, sitting on
walls. I tell Ruth to close the window.

I hear a snort of laughter from Aoife on the bed. I wait a
moment before going on.

– Then a town: on the outskirts of some town, in a garage,
Ruth comes back with a polystyrene cup of sweet tea. The
warm liquid dribbles into my stomach and I have to open the
door to vomit again. A young girl in the garage is watching
me from the window: I put my fingers down my throat and
wretch again for her benefit. Ruth buys me another bottle in
the town and then we follow the sea road, along high cliffs.
She is very quiet, too alert, constantly checking the mirrors.
Ruins crown the top of the hills all around us. I start touching

her as she drives, the soft white hair on her legs, pressing her breasts and then I find my way inside her underwear and put a finger into her. I regret this immediately: I know that it will lead to nothing but more frustration for both of us. My finger is inside her and I feel empty. She stays quiet when I take my hand away.

She wants to know what is wrong. We pass a set of electronic gates at the end of a long drive way. I drink some more whisky and this time Ruth joins with me without argument. The world through the windscreen is more solid and heavier and more garish than I've ever seen it. I want more than anything to close my eyes and sleep. Instead I start talking: I say anything that comes into my head—I don't know what I'm saying. About my older brother and a letter he once wrote me, about ships, about a tanker that arrived in the docks one day from Russia—anything. I shut up when I hear her gasp with pain and lean forward. She says she doesn't know what's the matter and gets out of the car in some flowery picnic area. There's a bench where she sits and bends over, rocking herself as the sun surrounds her. I see men in passing cars looking at her, some even slowing down.

The idea goes through my mind that I should leave her there, turn the key and abandon her there in a picnic area with its flowers and overflowing bins on a cliff. But it is the thought of the smiling man who will stop to give her a lift that paralyses me. I can see his hand on her thigh, the car stopping and Ruth closing her eyes as he slides over towards her. The sky is flooded with light reflected off the sea—shimmering and harsh.

Somehow, although I did not take my eyes off her while I was speaking, I missed Aoife move her hand from her breast to between her legs. Surreptitious or not, I can't decide. The other hand rested on her stomach, possibly as a shield to my eyes or she might have forgotten it for the moment. Her face is turned towards me in the candlelight, her eyes closed, a shadow obscuring her mouth.

– I try again against a wall behind the toilets, on the cliff edge, on the path down to the shingle shore. I can think of nothing else but fucking her, about why I can't. I am constantly molesting her as we walk along, her raw breasts, between her legs, her salt throat; I can't leave her alone, you see. We are both sore and on the verge of crying—a terrible dry wailing. We stumble along in the wind, supporting each other, falling down together. Ruth kneels at the edge of the water, clutching her stomach and vomits. The sea grabs at the ends of her hair. The sea moves in time with the pain in my groin. The light is comical and extravagant on us. We have given up trying to speak. At dusk, I grab her again near a shop, take her round the back between the bins and a pit of cinders. She doesn't even have the strength to resist as I pull the frock over her head. I can barely stand. Her silent eyes close, flicker open and she faints against me. I keep on at her nonetheless. Then a woman comes out the back door of the shop and sees us. She goes back in and I have to run, dragging Ruth, slapping her face, across a road to the shore, the woman and a man with a shotgun behind us.

– So why did he do it? Aoife is asking me. She has a firm hold of my arm. She is excitedly identifying things for me on the streets as we walk along. The house she was born in, her sister's first house when she married, the man who kept giant snails, all things I already know.

– You're giving me a commentary like I'm a stranger.

– Not like a stranger, she says elbowing me. I'm merely telling you again. What's wrong with that?

– Revenge, I say to her.

She stops abruptly and looks at me.

– Jimmy Caldwell, I remind her. The man we were talking about. He had his wee nephew push him around the streets at night in the wheelchair and Jimmy sprayed the messages on the walls. I doubt if Jimmy had any idea about the way things would turn out. It all came true.

– Is that an excuse? Aoife says, like she is asking herself. Before she has come to any decision, she says: You see that white door over there? That's where my friend used to live. My first boyfriend. Arnold he was called.

– Arnold Morrison, I remind her dryly.

– Can you believe it? How many Arnolds have you ever met? He had short spiky blond hair and a birthmark under his arm. He was knocked down one day and was in hospital for weeks. I got a friend of mine to jump on my leg to break it so I could see him.

– I know, I tell her.

Aoife laughs.

– It was mad. She only managed to sprain it though. Then when I got in to see him, he wouldn't talk to me. He told everyone it was my fault and I had pushed him. His parents threw me out of the hospital. They rang up mine as well and told them. And guess what? I admitted it.

Aoife buries her head, laughing into my shoulder.

– I admitted it.

Then I ask her a question I don't know the answer to already: Where did he go to anyway? This Arnold.

Aoife stops and looks at me as if I am joking. She lets herself go into another fit of laughter on my shoulder.

– Is he still around then? I try again but this makes it worse or funnier. A group of women talking in a doorway look over at us. Aoife won't stop laughing. I have to push her along the street.

– Where's this thing you want to show me anyway? I ask her but by the time she is calm enough to answer, we are already talking about something else.

– The pub was a long narrow room like a corridor. Ruth and I had nothing to say to each other. The stools and tables seemed to be too big for the place—made for some other kind of people than the shrunken old men around the bar. There were fag-burns on the ceiling. Ruth was shivering: her summer frock was torn at the shoulder and flecks of vomit and seasalt decorated her hair. I took her wrist and squeezed it as hard as I could; she looked at me wearily with her blue eyes. She was smoking a rolled cigarette she had gotten from one of the men at the bar. I squeezed her wrist until I saw the pain stirring in her eyes. A brown pube of tobacco stuck to her upper lip. At the bar, I stood between the old men and ordered shorts of whiskey—the old men's feet didn't reach the bottom rung of the high stools. There's no ice, the girl said and the shoulders of the old men shook silently; the girl had short dense curly hair like moss, a fat neck and a truculent red face—she might stick her tongue out at you at any minute.

One of the men was talking to Ruth. His head leaned down towards her hand like he wanted to lick her. He looked at me craftily, almost with a wink, a signal of our mutual lust. Ruth smiled and blushed, you see, when he lightly touched the rip in her summer frock with his smoke-browned finger. The warm whiskey was hard to swallow. I felt sick again. The back of my trousers were damp with sweat. I went to the toilet and the sour-faced barmaid followed me in, pulled down her jeans and let me at her from the back as she gripped the stone cistern. They were all huddled around Ruth at the table. In the tent later—Ruth put up the tent so we could try to sleep she said—I hadn't the strength to try again with her. She took off my trousers and I saw her gasp for breath after she caught the stench from my groin.

Talk to me about something, she said. I'm scared. Tell me a story. She put her arms around me and moved away again suddenly, as though she could sense the terrors in me. I had visions of deformed shadows gathering on the top of the dark hill. Ruth was crying beside me while the wind stamped around the grass. The nylon skin of the tent puckered and slapped like it was alive with rage. I saw things licking rocks and heard oaths made down in the earth. I longed for the morning—I said something to Ruth about waiting for the dawn. To calm myself, I tried to think about being younger, a boy, but it was as if my life was buried under some stone I lacked the strength to move. I felt her body stiffen, although I wasn't touching her. And it was then I heard a shout, followed by other voices. One side of the tent began to glow. They were shouting for me. They wanted Ruth: old men and young men. A bottle, it must have been a stone, hit the bar of the tent and skidded down the nylon. We were naked.

When I stop speaking, I notice that there is no sound of Aoife breathing. Her head is turned away from me on the bed and I wonder if she has fallen asleep at the same time as I am watching her hand at work on herself, kneading out her pleasure, the quickening and more impatient pace. She is near coming. Her body is straining imperceptibly, her shoulders tightened, her hips forced to stay down on the mattress. I want to call her name to let her know I am watching but my lips touch silently on the last syllable only; she hears the sound I make and responds with a low groan. I try another sound, a pain sound, a small injured gasp. Aoife lets out a long sigh of loneliness and that is followed by a cry like a child's. I breathe out heavily through my nose and make a brief angry grunting noise. Aoife hisses, as if she is laughing to herself. I find myself standing up to go over to her and have to force myself to sit back. She is quiet again. I feel a moment of stillness in the room and her hand has stopped moving.

– We run through the fields in the darkness, I carry on through the silence. I managed to grab some clothes—my trousers and a jumper which I give to Ruth. A mist is barely visible above the fields. They are chasing us: we can hear them laughing. At the car, we find out they have sliced the tyres. We follow the road, looking for a house, for lights, hoping a car will pass. Hi sexy, we're coming to get you, we can hear them shouting across the empty fields. Sexy: they are singing the word, drawing it out, contorting it, a chorus of men, Sexsiiieee—and there's a girl's voice amongst them. If we just keep running, the old ones will tire, I keep telling myself. Ruth runs silently beside me. Soon there's a stitch in my side. We pass an old hut and I pick up a piece of wood, but it's rotten and crumbles in my hand.

I catch a glimpse of the muck on Ruth's buttocks when we stop for a moment to try to catch our breath. We leave the road and head out into the fields. We climb over a loose stone wall which reminds me of the dark bare hill again. We can only run and run. The hunt for us seems to fall off. We get our second wind. A caravan—the half-demolished hull of a caravan dumped in the middle of nowhere. That's where we stop at last. Inside, the walls and roof are battered in; one of the windows has folded in on itself like a festered eye.

The place smells of animal and excrement. Ruth sits down in the darkest corner: I can't see her. I listen for her breathing. Something is scratching under the floor. What did they want? Ruth asks. I thought she was sleeping, you see. I find her in the corner and start kissing her—our mouths are utterly dry.

I realise that I want her again. She moans with reluctance but I pull her to her feet and drag the jumper over her head, put my mouth to her little breasts: her skin is cold and moist with sweat. She is shivering violently. I bite the bunched flesh above her hip and she grabs my head to protect herself, but then lets go. That feeling returns of not knowing what to do with her, that fucking her would be as light and brief a thing as touching her hair or wiping some dirt from her eyelid. I turn her around and around, the anger rising in me again. She is without will in my hands, lifeless and distant, and I leave her there in that sordid twisted shell of a holiday home. Naked and unused in the darkness: I leave her there alone. She doesn't call after me or try to follow. I go back across the fields, over the wall, back in the direction we had come from.

Holding my hand, Aoife brought me to the gates of the college and told me to climb over. We walked across the lawns until we reached a small path which took us under trees to a narrow gate in a row of hedges. Aoife went in first and carried on without me over the gravel towards a dark pond near a wall. I drifted in the other direction towards a doorless wooden shed. Inside were buckets and tins and a sleeping-bag spread on the ground. I heard Aoife call me. I was still annoyed by her strange behaviour, so I ignored her for a while and then walked slowly over. I had forgotten that she had brought me here for a reason.

 – There, she said, looking at the pond. The water was hidden below a layer of twisted roots and huge green leaves and rubbish. I found a stick and made a hole to see the water. It was black and shallow.

 – It's me, Aoife said.

I thought she was exaggerating again.

 – I'm broken, she added with a laugh.

– Is this what you wanted to show me? I said irritably.

She looked at me: her face was hostile and confused.

– That's me, she screamed and this time she pointed out over the fat crust on the water to a small statue I had not given any attention to. It was a young girl in grey stone, naked, her feet together and her hands joined above her head like she was waiting to dive. I looked closer at the face, short hair, close eyes—more like a boy's.

– The water is supposed to come out of my hands, I heard Aoife telling me. It's my body but somebody else's head.

– You never told me this before.

– I had to stand in a room for weeks and weeks. No clothes. My hands up. Days and days and days. I ran away and they caught me and brought me back. I think the feet are somebody else's too.

We stood on there and Aoife told me more about the artist, an old man. I said we should steal it, we should take the statue home and Aoife seemed to like the idea until I had my shoes and socks off and was about to go into the water. For some reason then, she changed her mind and put her hand on my shoulder. She looked away when I tried to speak to her. I went back over to the shed with my shoes in my hand.

The Beauty of Restraint

One night when he was out walking he saw a group of children and they were running naked down the back lanes. On another night he saw a street light slowly lean over and fall in an empty street. On the Letterkenny Road, near dawn, he encountered an old woman who clutched his hand and talked nonsense and he left her there. He found an artificial eye outside a bar in the centre of town—the glass was cracked. Up along the Culmore Road, he stepped on a soldier's beret and felt his heart subside at the thought that it was a small animal or even a child wrapped in a blanket. Walking the streets at night he had seen foxes and men too drunk to move, young couples in the grass on the embankment, rioting crowds, lights flashing in obsolete houses. But mostly, on these walks, Henry O'Hagan saw nothing.

Then, on a stormy night in October, Henry O'Hagan turned the corner of William Street and was stopped by the sight of a dog dragging itself into a doorway. The dog's spine seemed to be damaged, the back legs buckled and useless. The street was littered with bricks and smashed glass after the teatime riot. But then the rain had grown heavier and they had all probably decided to stay in for the night. Henry waited until the soaking animal had reached the shelter of the doorway. He waited some more while the dog held him in its weak gaze and once he saw the eyes close with exhaustion, he wrapped the animal in his coat and carried it home.

Henry O'Hagan lived in a bare stone house on Rosemount Avenue, opposite the post office. The windows were filthy and weeds and moss overflowed the ledges and gutters like green snow. The houses on either side were bright and painted: to the left lived Danny Pierce, with his wife and four sons, and on the other side lived the Youngs, who have now all moved to Australia. The neighbours looked on Henry O'Hagan as a lonely but harmless man, a man who did not seem to change or age, like they knew they had themselves, who never answered the knock on his door because he knew it would be only the children teasing him. Even so, they felt responsible for him in some indefinable way. On the night of the fire in the Youngs', once the children were safe, Danny Pierce and Buttons Young kicked in the front door and carried Henry O'Hagan out into the street. It was four in the morning. Not only was O'Hagan still dressed, his face was thickly coated in shaving foam. At the sight of him, the children jumped to the worst conclusion: now when the story is told, Danny and Buttons are celebrated for saving O'Hagan from a raging inferno, the skin on him bubbling and dropping off in disgusting white lumps. Of course, now, there are some who say that Henry O'Hagan should have been left in that building until he was ashes, like everything else that never quite belonged to him.

Henry laid the dog on a blanket on the floor, lit a fire and sat in his chair. The thing was a mongrel, some terrier, maybe even a bit of spaniel. One ear was black and the other brown, sagging ears that seemed out of proportion with the lean and short-haired, white body. There was another spot of black at the joint of its left front leg. Gazing at the steam rising from the animal's wet fur, Henry began to speculate about what he was going to do with this wounded creature. He checked again for a collar and began to pace the room, trying to imagine where the dog lived and if it had an owner. It was clear to him the animal wasn't starved and there was no sign of maltreatment other than the confusing trouble with its hind legs. Perhaps the dog had been hit by a car or a badly thrown brick or even struck by a plastic bullet in the riot earlier. There had been so many stories recently of heroic animals throwing themselves in the path of some missile or other intended for their human master. And there were also stories of traitorous animals: dogs thought lost or dead, reappearing out of the back of army saracens.

For the following two days the dog lay almost dead on the blankets on the floor of the front room. Occasionally, it would stir and try to sit up and Henry would jump out of his chair shouting encouragement. Henry forgot all about his nocturnal walks. The hours passed, the fire would shrink into the dark and the morning splattered against the window like a bucket of water. On the third day, the dog opened its small black eyes and stared at him. A full day passed like that. Henry offered the animal scraps of bacon, bread in milk, a raw egg, to no avail. The next day he made up his mind and walked down into the centre of town in search of the vet's clinic only to discover that it had been burned out the night before in a wilder than usual bout of rioting.

Henry O'Hagan realised with a shock that he was almost happy about this act of mindless hooliganism and stopped at the butcher's for some oxtail which he seemed to be remember drove dogs mad with delight, the thick tough bone, the shreds of meat clinging to the crevices. He put the bone in front of the sleeping dog and went out again, back into the area of William Street, where he checked the windows of the remaining shops for any notice of a missing dog. He went into the local bar and ordered a pint. The barman looked like a greyhound, Henry found himself thinking, a cross-eyed greyhound with a red bow tie. Henry tried to start a conversation about the recent trouble and casually recalled the sight of a dog crawling on its belly a few nights before. The barman shook his head sadly and said he hated to see an animal in pain. Henry wondered aloud what might have happened to the animal but the barman merely shrugged and switched on the TV on the shelf for the racing results.

That night Henry decided he had done as much as anyone could and went out for a walk. The night was clear, a strangely high and cloudless sky above the frosted fields. He headed up into the hills, but even there under the stars he could not stop thinking about the dog in his front room and that at any moment it might raise its head and see the empty chair and decide enough was enough and fall asleep for good. He hurried home. The relief he felt on seeing the blanket gently rising and falling, on hearing the animal snort and cough, at the sour aroma of urine in the room was almost enough to stop his own breathing and he had to stand in the backyard for a few minutes to calm himself down. Later that night as he tried to change the blanket, Henry noticed the dog was bleeding from its rear end. He took the oxtail bone into the kitchen to inspect it for teethmarks but it had not been touched.

On Sunday morning, although it made him anxious to leave the dog by itself, Henry was there as usual at eight o' clock mass at the end of a bench near the altar. Mrs Fannon occupied the other end, with a nauseated grimace on her face as she counted the decades of her four sets of rosary beads. Fr Hegarty, a young priest with a rural accent and round glasses, talked about the ugliness of excess and the patience of Job. Henry stared at the red light suspended before the tabernacle and prayed wordlessly for the dog. At communion time, as he always did, he helped Mrs Fannon up to altar. Then, as the priest approached him, Henry found himself doing something he had never done before, never even thought about—he held out his hands to take the Host. The people on either side of him turned and stared, the red-haired altar boy seemed to smirk and Fr Hegarty himself hesitated with the sacrament between his fingers. Henry lowered his eyes, to the tacks embedded in the green matting on the altar and Mrs Fannon's bruised and bloated ankles tied up like meat in the blue strings of her veins.

Instead of rushing straight home, Henry found himself walking aimlessly along the gravel paths in the park. The old leaves blew around him in the blasts of wind. Once or twice he held his hands before his face and looked at them closely as if they were asking him some question. He watched the crows jumping about on the bare branches as though they were also trying to attract his attention. Even the exposed root of an old sycamore, thick and black and buckled, seemed to be grumbling something to him. He stared at himself in a big puddle and saw the clouds gently colliding behind him. When the park filled with people on their way to the next mass, Henry followed them. It was a much slower mass; Fr Thornton spoke and moved around the altar like a man trying to pretend he was alone. Again Henry joined the queue for communion and again he held out his cupped hands. As he turned away from the altar, he mimed putting the Host in his mouth, and walked back to his seat. He made himself stay until the very end of mass with the white disc pressed between his palms, staring at the long red light on its chains behind the priest. No one paid him any attention as he went out again into the cold and windy morning.

Danny Pierce was out on his front step considering the weather. He was worried. He was waiting on his pigeons returning. The cloud was gathering and the strengthening south-westerly wind would hamper the birds flying home into the north. Danny was trying out a new bird he had great hopes for.

– They'll be battered coming over the mountains, Danny observed aloud as he noticed someone passing. He spoke without discrimination or intention; anyone going by, man, woman or child, might have stopped and wondered if it was really them he was talking to because his eyes remained fastened on the sky. His neighbours knew to avoid him on race days since he might become suddenly irascible and paranoid. His wife, Mona, took the children to her mother's for their dinner.

– Aw, it's you Henry, he said. You can't sneak by me that easy y'know. What d'ye think? I've a great bird up there the day. It's first outing. It'll beat the arse off anything flying out this town so it will. Mark my words.

Henry nodded, eager to get back inside, nervous about the contraband in his pocket.

– Ye alright there, Henry? You look a bit under the weather there. You'd need to be careful. Remember this time last year. Eh?

Henry had been through this many times before so he was not surprised that Danny was able to see the state he was in. He took the house keys noisily out of his pocket as a polite sign that he had no time to linger. He glanced conspiratorially at the sky and nodded again.

– Aye, remember that day, Henry, said Danny, swivelling his head to a different part of the sky. We thought we'd lost you there. You'd need to watch that heart of yours. You've been warned once. You'll end up lying in the road again like last year. I'll tell you something, Henry, Danny sighed and studied the sky over the brown empty hills, between you and me: I'll be the one collapsing in the road if that cock of mine doesn't show itself pretty soon.

While Danny suffered his intimations of defeat, Henry quickly inserted his key in the door and escaped inside. Without any more delay, he knelt beside the wheezing dog, broke the Host into four pieces and laid it by the dog's snout. The dog opened an eye and watched him, sniffed at the white biscuit and cast a weary look at its strange protector. The bleeding seemed to have stopped but the animal appeared weaker than ever before, panting for no purpose, the legs trembling. Henry thought for a while and then carefully opened the dog's jaw. The breath smelled like a freshly dug road. The two blunted tawny incisors reminded him of the sawn-off slabs at the border. Then Henry took a piece of the bread and laid it on the dog's tongue. The animal seemed to wretch, unable to swallow. Henry dribbled some water from his fingers into its mouth. Then he broke what was left into smaller pieces and patiently knelt by the dog's head until only a few crumbs lay in the palm of his hand which he licked away.

That same Sunday, Henry also made it in time for the 12.30 mass. He was there again for the 7 the next morning, the 11 also, and the 7.30. To avoid drawing attention to his new-found piety, he began to use chapels in other parts of the city; he made the journey up to Creggan, Pennyburn, out to Galliagh and even discovered a small draughty chapel up the Culmore Road that did mass at odd times. Back in his front room, Henry knelt by the dog and repeated the process of feeding it the crumbled Host.

After a week, he came in the front door and saw the dog trying to raise itself up on its front legs. This time, Henry stood back silently in the shadows and watched. A few days later, the animal was able to lift the front half of its body and stretch its back end without any sign of pain.

The dog's appetite soon returned. Henry bought the best

meat and even paid a visit to the library to look up information on calcium and protein. The dog's rekindled interest in food made life much easier for Henry; he planted pieces of the Eucharist in the marrow of bones, dissolved it in broth and stock, sprinkled it on canned dog food, fried it with bits of kidney. Every day the dog seemed to be getting better. Whenever Henry entered the room, the dog's clipped tail stood erect. But even so, the animal never once approached Henry for a pat or a carry-on the way dogs usually do. Henry put this down to the animal's innate sense of pride; being sick is a process of humiliation, Henry reminded himself. People come to see you to ponder your degradation, to affirm what they already know about their own death, not for any other benevolent reason. Henry knew all about this from his month in hospital the year before after a mild heartache. He remembered lying on the street unable to move, gripped by a pain that was more than physical. The children gathered around and taunted him, asked him what he was looking for, if there was a bad smell down there, thinking the stupid old man had fallen over on the street.

Another week went by and Henry decided it might be a good idea to give the dog some fresh air. It wouldn't do any harm at least, he told himself. He waited until well after midnight to avoid attracting attention. He knew people would talk if they came upon him with a dog. In the kitchen he found a piece of cord in a drawer he could use as a tether. The night was cold, so cold the air seemed stalled and lost on the streets. A white powder lay along the roads and roofs. When Henry looked back to check that they had not been seen, he noticed that the only tracks in the frost were his own. The dog looked strangely serious, almost solemn, and held its head poised and alert.

– What's wrong there, boy? Henry said to the animal. Ye

134

worried I'm going to take ye back? No one wants you, boy. No one wants either of us. We can do whatever we want. Y'know, there's some call that freedom.

Henry heard himself laughing on the hushed street. The dog looked up at him.

– What's the matter? Never heard me laugh before. And d'ye know what else? We're going to have to give you a name. How's about that for a laugh and a half?

As they walked through the streets and out of the town, Henry tried out all the names he could think of. None of them seemed to do the trick for him and the dog showed no response to any he said aloud.

– Well, not everything needs a name, Henry said eventually, and sighed, and the sigh hung before him in the air like a frail and miniature ghost with nowhere to go and he closed his eyes as he passed through it.

On the fringes of the town, out among the hills and the occasional farm, the dog stopped at a bend in the road. Henry stepped back and waited, thinking the creature might want to have a sniff at something or take a piss. In the trees to one side, he noticed a dark and narrow opening which he soon realised was the beginning of a lane he had never spotted before. Henry wondered aloud to the dog about where the path might take a soul and the dog lifted its face and looked at him, and carried on looking at him until he felt he was being stared at or even scrutinised. Henry felt himself shiver. He gave the lead a tug and tried to move on but the dog stayed where it was, looking up at him. For a terrible moment, Henry imagined there were more sets of eyes watching him in the darkness. He found himself loosening his grip on the cord wrapped around his wrist. Perhaps the animal knows this place, Henry started to think, maybe the dog has been here before and had brought him here for a reason. He took a step back from the animal and let the end of the leash drop on the ground between them. The animal turned and watched him with blank, heavy eyes, like it was staring at him and falling asleep at the same time. Henry stamped his feet and tried to calm his breathing. The weight of the muck on his boots worried him. He stepped further back. How far to the nearest house? he heard himself wonder. He thought about Mrs Fannon's swollen ankles at the altar.

First thing the next morning, Henry went down to Huttons, the pet shop, and bought the strongest leash and collar. The leash was made of woven strips of coarse leather and it had four studs like small metallic pyramids. He attended mass at the Long Tower, received communion and then signed on. On his way home, he saw the carcass of a cat lying at the gates of the library. He turned the body over with his foot and there was a wet stain on the ground. Even the dead cast a shadow, he said to himself.

The dog watched him from the doorway as he fried some gristles in the kitchen. Henry emptied the metal chain and the collar out of the bag onto the kitchen floor. The dog retreated into the living room, whining.

– You'll not do that again, he said to the animal. He remembered the anger and fear of the night before when he had turned and walked away from the dog on the country road. He had walked as fast as he could through the darkened lanes, telling himself not to run because that would be to lose control of the situation. He was back on the streets before he heard the scuffing paws and breathing at his side and there was the dog strolling along as though it had been there all along.

While the dog was eating the gristles, Henry looked again at the collar with its silver name-tag, a blank disc on a ring between two of the big studs. The metal was smoother and softer than any knife. He watched his own reflection disappear when he breathed on it. Out the window in the backyard, the pigeons were pecking at the moss and strutting about importantly. He opened the back door and the pigeons lifted into the air like a big magnet had pulled them all upwards at once. The sun appeared, white and low, from behind the clouds. He went back inside and returned with a saucer where he had broken up the Host when he was frying. He lifted the saucer up to his mouth and blew the remains into the yard. From the window, he watched the pigeons come down one by one through the sunshine to peck and fight over the white crumbs.

Henry was now attending mass four or five times a day. The dog seemed improved every time he looked at it—the sheen had come back to its coat. Henry had decided to stop taking communion himself. He never wondered why he had ceased to receive the holy bread; it was just one of those things that happened to him, the way most of his life seemed to have happened to him without him feeling either surprised, thankful or disappointed. These thoughts came one damp and dreary day in February while he was passing time in the park until the next mass in the cathedral. He was watching the ducks in the winter pond; the water was greasy and thick. One of the ducks approached, pushing itself with effort, a brown one, moving to and fro at his feet in a weak effort at exhibitionism. Henry smiled: keeping his hand in his pocket, he broke up the Host from the last mass in Galliagh and sprinkled the pieces on the water. The duck scooped them up after a show of disinterest. The others sailed slowly across to him, bending their necks, quacking doubtfully.

In the days that followed, Henry began to distribute the Eucharist wherever he went. To the stray dogs in the streets. At nights he would leave some for the cats. He fed the ducks in the

137

park, the showers of sparrows, the crows, the gangs of seagulls along the river and opened his hand on the bridge to feed the fishes. He did not forget Danny's pigeons which now regularly congregated in his backyard. He left some for the mice behind the skirting board in the kitchen. He planted a whole piece in the forest floor where he believed he had once seen a deer. Most of the fields were empty but he managed to find some sheep and a small herd of friendly cows. Once he lifted part of a paving stone which had been smashed for missiles in a riot and he gave to the insects, to the sombre, moist ground itself.

Of course, the increasing scale of his administrations required constant attendance at mass around the city and a greater risk of being caught. Henry felt he did not have a moment to himself. One evening, as he was pretending to put the Eucharist in his mouth at the altar, the bread slipped between his fingers and floated down to the stone floor. Henry froze, as did everyone else. They all stared at the small white medallion at their feet. The red-haired altar boy came across the hoovered carpet to see what was going on. Henry seemed to be nodding to himself as though he was affirming privately that his life had been destined for this moment and now everything made sense. Perhaps it was his nodding that infuriated the priest, Fr Hegarty, who pushed Henry aside and got down on his knees to retrieve the fallen sacrament, blowing on it as though it was hot. Henry went back to his seat without waiting to be offered another try.

One afternoon as he was feeding the pigeons in his back yard, Henry was surprised by Danny's head appearing over the wall.

– How's the form there, Henry?

Henry stiffened, closed his hands into fists and put them behind his back. The birds continued pecking at the white flakes around his feet.

– What'd I tell you eh? said Danny. What'd I tell you, Henry?

Henry looked at Danny's unshaven face above the coloured fins of glass along the top of the wall. Henry feared the worst. His skull seemed to tighten inside his skin. He opened his mouth, but had no idea what to say. His eyes stung as if he was facing a bright light. At his feet he heard the birds humming and scuffling.

– Look at him, said Danny, rearranging his feet on the stool he was standing on. Look at the pride in him. The way he thinks he runs the whole show. Look at the intelligence. You can see it jist looking at him. The swagger. Loftiness. D'you get it? Loft - iness. I bet you that's where the word comes from. I bet you.

Henry blinked away the glare of shame and followed Danny's gaze to a pigeon strutting around in front of the back gate.

– A full hour he came in front of the rest of them. Unheard of, they're saying. Hoax. Cheat. Fix, they're all saying. A big fix, Danny laughed and then he cupped his hand around his mouth and roared out, Youse are all jist jealous.

Henry put his hands in his pockets and did his best to smile.

– Well done, he managed to say.

– Aye, well they seem to be getting to know you a bit anyway, Henry. I see them gathering in here more. What's that you're giving them anyway? Just a bit of bread?

Henry found himself nodding.

– Aye but not too much. It's a misconception y'know, this bread stuff. A wee bit of corn's good for them. I'll tell you what's really good for them though. Full of nutritional value. Brick. Red brick.

Henry made a face that was somewhere between surprise and fear.

– I'm telling you. People wouldn't believe you, Danny went on. You might as well tell them God is a banana bloody skin. Pulverised red brick. I'm not codding you. Y'see them street pigeons hanging around on the roofs and windowsills an'all? What are they up to? They're eating the place from under us. Take it from me. Nibbling away so they are. A wee bit at a time. Like that story, y'know, where the wee bird has to move this mountain of sand a grain at a time. Y'know the one I mean? Everyone knows it.

Henry shook his head and shrugged.

– Aye, but y'know what I'm on about, said Danny, feeling annoyed for some reason. It's a good story so it is. Have a look for it in the library or something so you should.

Danny fell quiet as he looked at his neighbour nodding and shifting his stance in the backyard. Henry O' Hagan was always a well-turned-out man, thought Danny to himself, a tall man, always the suit and tie and the hair flattened on his head. But he had seen better days. There was a definite yellowness about his neighbour. On the skin. The gills. And the eyes were too dim. Weak. The man wasn't well. Maybe that was a bad idea to mention the story of that wee bird, he wondered. Danny wasn't certain, but he thought he remembered the story had to do with dying.

– D'ye ever wonder about hibernation, Henry? Danny said, trying to change the subject. Y'know, why we don't an'all?

Danny was interrupted here by his wife calling from the kitchen that there was a reporter on the phone for him.

– I can't cope with this life of stardom at all, Henry, he said as he disappeared with a wink of his eye behind the wall.

– Sex, drugs and rock'n'roll—here I come, Henry heard him saying in a big American voice and then the door slammed.

Snow fell every day for the next week. The few with work

didn't bother going in. The bread was hard in the shops. The schools closed and the streets were full of children in coats. With their reddened hands and faces, they might have all been victims of some strange contagion. Behind the noise of their shouts, there was a deep and sometimes anxious silence. The riots died off and the barricades were sprinkled with talcum powder. At night, on his walks with the dog, now that Henry never ventured out into the back roads, the phosphorescent barricades appeared at the ends of streets like the carcasses of prehistoric animals.

At the end of that week, 27 February, Henry was sitting on a bench in the park in a bunker of snow. The sky was now a clear undamaged blue. He was studying the pattern of his own footprints as they came up the hill and through the bare trees towards him. Something in the sight of his own tracks in the snow gave him comfort in his heart. They'll be gone soon, he told himself, and smiled. The last few mornings he had not being feeling so well, a sense of fatigue deep inside him he could not get rid of, a breathlessness. He tried to tell himself it was the weather, the cold. But he knew it was the exertion of getting to all those masses, and the strain and worry that he might be caught.

He got to his feet and made his way through the crisp snow to the pond. Hemmed in by ice, a single duck floated in the centre of the pond in a small pool of water. Henry put the toe of his boot to the ice and pressed. There was a series of small cracks and the water seeped up. He walked further round the edge and found a branch and pressed it down carefully through the ice until he felt the bottom. But the ice was too thin and when he let go, the stick fell over like a lamp-post one time. A curled slither of bark stuck to his hand. He put it to his lips, touched the damp wood with the tip of his tongue. It tasted how it looked, brown and moist and decaying. He crunched it between his teeth and swallowed. Henry had to try a number of times before all the bark went down his throat. Then he took the Eucharist out of his pocket.

– There's only one of you, so you can't have all of it, he said to the duck which was facing the other way.

Suddenly, he felt a fist slamming between his shoulder blades, like a thump exploding. As he turned to see what was going on, he was hit in the face. First there was a sharp pain but then a sense of spreading cold. He wiped the snow off his face. Over under the trees, four young lads were ready for him.

– Come on, ya aul loony, they were shouting.

One of them launched another snowball which hit Henry on the knee. Three more followed and Henry's hat was knocked off his head. He looked at it lying there in the snow and remembered the soldier's beret from a night a long time before.

– Come on ya aul loony headcase, they were shouting, daring him to fight back. The loudest of them was a lad with red hair who Henry thought he knew from somewhere, perhaps just around the streets. The grass appeared in appalling clarity where the boys scooped up the snow.

– Hi Henry, the red-head shouted. Leave them ducks alone. I'm warning ye. They're not doing ye any harm. Yer not allowed to chat up the ducks now so yer not.

Henry was too slow to react. He could see the boy's arm going back, the tightening face, the thick wet red hair and the white ball rising through the air, but the thing was in his face before he could move out of the way. The four lads shouted and cheered.

– Chat that one up, ya headbanger.

Henry decided the best thing to do was to get away from them. He started walking as quickly as he could up the steps and along another path to the nearest gate. The lads came after him and the snowballs pounded against his back and smashed into pieces on the ground around him.

– Hi Henry. Henry, ye forgot yer hat. Henry, here's yer hat.

Henry started to run. He tried to cross the grass and slipped, but managed to get up again. The snowballs seemed to be coming from all directions. He thought about the dog, wondered what it would do in this situation; if it would protect him or stand and watch indifferently or even hungrily as the boys tormented him. He ran on, gasping for breath, his eyes and nose streaming. He was running the wrong way. There was no gate this way; only an old green house in the corner where the park attendants kept their tools. He reached the wall and put his hands against the stone as though it could be pushed aside. He made to move to the left but now two of the lads had got in front of him and were blocking his way. The other two waited behind him. They began to pelt him with snowballs.

– D'ye want yer hat or not, Henry?

Henry opened his eyes and saw the red-haired lad moving towards him, a step at a time.

– What's the matter with ye, Henry? We're jist trying to give yer hat back and yer doing all this hiding. We're jist trying to do ye a good turn. A wee touch of Christian charity. If ye don't take it, Henry, we're going to think yer wile ungrateful so we are.

Henry held out his hand for the hat, closing his eyes again to whatever they were going to do to him.

There was only silence. For a second or two, Henry thought he was dead. A knife through the heart. A bullet to the head. Instant death. There was not a sound anywhere in the world. He wondered about the dog; who would look after it. Then he was shocked by a deafening crunching noise and imagined walking across a field of bones. It was their feet in the snow, he realised, and the sound was moving away from him. Even then he kept his eyes closed, even when he could no longer hear them, and a crow was gurgling in a tree nearby.

He didn't move, his back against the wall and his frozen hand held out to the world. His trousers stuck to his legs. He tried to concentrate on the numbness in his fingertips. Finally, he opened his eyes to the brightness of the whitened park. He didn't recognise the place. The trees were gnarled and broken veins in the sky. His hat was there like a carcass in the snow. Then he saw the Eucharist lying unbroken in his open palm.

Henry O'Hagan might not have seen much of the world but he knew that the truth quickly becomes a rumour because rumours are easier to believe. He knew he was in big trouble. As fast as he could, he headed home and bolted the front door. The dog was covered in ashes from rolling in the fireplace. It ran in circles around the front room as if it wanted to be chased. Henry stood for a while watching the streets through the window. Eventually, the dog gave up and lay down in a corner with one eye open. Henry pulled the curtains and checked the back door.

In the kitchen, he searched in the cupboards to see what they had left. A tin of peas, two sausages, no potatoes, one egg, a few wrinkled carrots, butter, half a loaf. He had meant to do some shopping. He emptied his pockets onto the mantelpiece. Along with the blue balls of fluff and a safety pin, there were two old wafers of holy bread. He picked some specks of dirt from them, blew on them to remove the dust, and put each one side by side around the rim of the mirror on the wall.

– We'll be hibernating now all right, he said to the dog.

The dog sneezed and scratched its snout with the back of its paw. Henry sat down in his chair, feeling the stiff fabric of his trousers against his knees. Soon enough it grew dark, then darker. The dog waited by the door, swiping its head now and again at the leash which was hanging from the door handle. Henry was too tired to explain. To the sound of the chain jangling, he closed his eyes and saw something bright and round and shining in the darkness. At first he thought it was a coin, but as it came closer he saw that it was a disc of very smooth metal. Peering even closer, he felt his heart quicken and ache at the sight of this thin pendant of metal. There was not the slightest mark or scratch on it. He had never seen anything so smooth and so perfect. Then, before his eyes, he saw his own name appear on the silver wafer. The dog watched him and growled.

Young Matthew Toner lost no time before informing his mother of what he had seen nestled in Henry O'Hagan's palm in the park. He was just passing, he told his mother, him and his pals, playing in the snow and they went over to see the ducks and out of the blue Henry appeared and asked them if they wanted to see something special. Matthew's mother, to give her credit, knew the like of her son and put it to him that they were tormenting the poor man and what would anybody be doing with the holy sacrament in the park in weather like this. Young Matthew started to cry because his mother wouldn't believe him. Mrs Toner gave him a slap around the head and threw him back out in the snow until he got a grip on himself.

Nevertheless, later in the day, she happened to mention the story to John Plunkett in the shop; Plunkett repeated it to his wife in bed for the sake of something to talk about and she then brought it into work with her the next morning to the sacristy, to the bad luck of Henry O'Hagan. Within an hour, Fr Hegarty had heard the story of the diabolical offer in the park and the fear and terror of the young boys. Now Fr Hegarty, being a young priest, tried not to jump to conclusions with much less will than he made up his mind about things. His mind was tormented with vague images of lewd acts conducted in the vicinity of the holy bread. Immediately

145

after his last service, he made the journey through the snow up the Academy Road and knocked on Henry's front door. He got no response but he happened to meet Danny coming back from the pigeon club with a basketful of birds. Danny invited the shivering priest in for a cup of tea and heard the story about his neighbour for the first time. Together with his wife, they tried to answer the priest's questions about Henry, his family and his habits. They couldn't help much but they were both adamant that Henry was a decent man. Later that night in bed, Danny had a terrifying dream of demon pigeons filling the skies and plucking the hearts out of innocent children on the street.

Over the next few weeks Fr Hegarty knocked on Henry O'Hagan's door so many times he lost count. It seemed impossible to catch the man at any time of day or night. There were never any lights on in the house either. The neighbours on the other side were now on constant look-out and it wasn't long before the whole neighbourhood of Rosemount knew that the clergy were searching for Henry O'Hagan. There was even talk of a reward for any information. Eventually, Fr Hegarty came to the conclusion that his prey had gone underground or on the run and was adjusting himself to his disappointment that he had missed the chance of an important confrontation with the realms below. It has to be said that Danny Pierce played a crucial part in all this; everywhere he went, he argued for Henry's innocence, said he was being scapegoated because he was a bit odd and lost no opportunity to remind people of the untrustworthiness of young Toner's word. Here again, fortune seemed to be against Henry. A young girl was found murdered in a field and the crucifix she should have been wearing was discovered by the autopsy to be lodged deep inside her. Fr Hegarty went back to Henry's door in a frenzied state of mind.

Fr Hegarty had another priest with him whose name or face no one knew, a tall thin man with a clipped beard. A small crowd gathered in the street to watch. Word went round that the letterbox was sealed shut. Danny was in position at his own door, berating the priests and the tribementality of his neighbours. The two priests took turns at knocking as though it could be done in an infinite number of ways. In the end, Nettles Ward, who was just passing, was pushed forward as someone who might know how to open a locked door with the least amount of fuss.

The stench was Fr Hegarty's first impression of the inside of the house: a stale sleepy odour that made him dizzy. Once he grew used to the smell, it was the growling of some animal in the darkness he noticed. He found a door at his right hand in the hall and, taking a deep breath, he threw it open. For a moment he thought it was a wardrobe or an airing cupboard he was looking into, but then his eyes discovered the source of the snarling and he made out the dull white pallor of the dog and two glistening, leering eyes. He checked behind him for the other priest—a Fr Hugh—blessed himself and stepped carefully into the room. The dog lowered its chest to the ground, bearing its teeth. Fr Hegarty moved farther in, slowly taking off his coat which he thought he could throw over the dog if it made any attempt on him. With his back along the wall, he made a circumference of the room, one eye on the dog, unsure what the other eye was looking for.

At the window, he reached behind him and pulled the curtains apart. A thick light from the street fought its way through the filthy dark in the room and gave up at the feet of the dog. In the shadow behind the animal, Fr Hegarty saw what he thought must be an armchair and he was certain there was someone sitting in it. His mouth seemed to be full of a disgusting mush as he tried to call Henry's name. Outside

147

in the street, he could hear the voices of the growing crowd. Suddenly he began to worry about what he was doing in this house. What if this was an entirely innocent man, who was sleeping easily in his chair—would these people be satisfied? He would be made to look a fool, if they didn't lynch him themselves. He moved too quickly and the dog raised its head at him. There was a bone on the floor beside it.

He didn't see what happened next but it must have been that Fr Hugh came up on the animal from behind, threw a blanket over it and hit the animal on the head with a shovel he had picked up from somewhere. Fr Hegarty immediately stepped over the lump under the coat and approached the chair. Again he was unable to say the man's name. Fr Hugh now pulled the curtains apart properly and they both saw the face of a man asleep in his chair. The rest of him however was gorged and pulled apart. Parts of his stomach lay in his lap. The legs were gone from the knee down. Fr Hegarty turned his eyes away and caught sight of his own reflection in a mirror on the wall. There were two round white medals inserted in the rim which he studied without recognising.

Henry O'Hagan was eaten by the dog he had taken in off the streets and reared back to good health. Fr Hegarty did not say that. Fr Hegarty refused to say anything at all to the people outside that night, or the night after, and in fact for nearly two years afterwards it was hard to get a decisive word out of Fr Hegarty without the accompanying disclaimer of 'How would I know anyway?' or 'Why are you asking me for?'

It was actually Danny who got to the bottom of the matter. He went over the back wall of his own house and, while the two priests were picking up the pieces and arranging for an ambulance, Danny found himself with a good view through the back window on the situation in the living room. Danny was quick to see that the best way he could protect himself and uphold the champion quality of his best bird was if what he was seeing through the window was allowed to become common knowledge. People would be so appalled and disgusted that Danny's reputation would not be under any threat. So, understanding all this in an instant, Danny made his apologies to the ghost of Henry O'Hagan and rushed back out to the street to let people know what he had seen.

No one knew where the dog had come from but neither were they sure if Henry had owned a dog all along. The animal recovered from the blow from the spade but was put down within a day or two and buried in a field over the border, by Fr Hegarty himself, they say, because Fr Hegarty would not give a straight answer. Henry O'Hagan, on the other hand, was buried in the cemetery, watched by an unusually big crowd, none of whom had a bad word to say about him. People wept and said they were missing him around the place already and it was agreed by all that it was tragic and unnecessary to die like that at only fifty-eight years of age, no matter how odd you were. Some of the older ones recalled stories of an overbearing mother and there was mention of a wayward brother across the water who didn't have the decency to show his face.

Danny was there also, if only in body, because he was severely distracted by the news that his bird had not even finished in the top three in the race that weekend. Strange and uncanny notions were forming in his head and he felt irritable every time he laid eyes on a priest.

The Good News

Hanley was spotted running around in the fog. He was running around and laughing and shouting in the square—at the walls, the emptied buildings. He was clapping his hands. There was squabbling and jabbing among the birds on the tower which he looked up at, and then he disappeared in the fog. He came back into sight running across the square with Zenny Kelly—the last of the name—wandering behind with his arms held out like there was still hope. Hanley hid up against the wall. Zenny stumbled on and fell and got up again and went down for good under the fog. The birds stirred on the slopes of the tower and some lifted and swooped. Hanley climbed a bit of wall and jumped down again and ran to the corner of Strand and hid in there in a door.

Once there was a bakery on Strand and that's where Curtsy Shields sleeps in the old oven. Curtsy was stretching himself and cursing out in the morning air and Hanley clapped his hands across the way in the fog. We all know Curtsy—he talks without restraint but claims to remember nothing. When he thumped on the door of the Ditch, it was a long time before any of us would listen to him. It was more time still before he was believed.

Curtsy told us that Hanley sat behind the wheel of a wreck on Strand and pretended to be going somewhere, steering and swerving. He got out and pulled open the boot and some thing like a snake reared up and licked the fog. Then Hanley went behind the buildings to the river and away from there again into Sand Street—like he was confirming the river was there yet. For a long while he leaned against a wall, for no good reason in Curtsy's opinion. Hanley took the hill up to Abercorn and the alley after that and out underneath the giant trellis woven out of the debris of the city and higher than—Alta says there will be nothing higher by the time they're done. In the end they came to Mill Street and Curtsy told us the fog was thinning and Hanley stopped and knocked on a window. Curtsy decided on the spot that enough was enough and ran the length of the way back and punched on the silver door of the Ditch.

Jimmy Mulvey got up on a table and quietened the din of us. Some were wondering what it was all about and who this Hanley was—the younger ones didn't know the name. Jimmy Mulvey stood on the table and banged his hammers on the ceiling.

– I was there thon day. I saw it. We all saw it. We buried him. Aye, this Hanley. That was ten years ago, yousens. We put him under. Hear that.

A crowd ganged up on the door to get out. There was a scrap in the corner and that ended with Wee Frankie Wells being killed, which brought us all some peace. Jimmy said some words about Wee Frankie and ordered his body to be taken out. The feet were no sooner through the door and the scraping and shouting started again. Jimmy threw the hammers around the place—Indian and NoNails blocked the door. Ones wanted to go straight out and grab Hanley but Jimmy was—Jimmy thought there would be no benefit and shouted that there were things to find out first. Not many cared and wanted to get Hanley back in the ground and they climbed up on the tables—Yelter, Larry FitzGrade, Brian Heights, they all got up on the tables and said there was nothing to find out.

– He's dead and that's your lot. He shouldn't be here—
that's what they were shouting around and ones cheering and
agreeing.

– I know him, Jimmy was shouting back. I went round with
him. There was once and we were out by the castle, just me
and him. There was this storm and we were there trapped for
two days. You couldn't see. There was no point. We got back
and they were all suspicious and thought we had done something or went some place. Somewhere. They locked us up.
Hear that.

We were all looking at him telling us this which wasn't like
Jimmy—the hammers were up each side of his face like he
would crush his own head if he wasn't heard. It brought the
order back—the sight of him roaring and remembering.
Jimmy got down from the table and took his time to pick
three of us to go out with him and establish if it was all happening like Curtsy was saying and where Hanley was. Curtsy
was over against the wall showing ones how Hanley clapped
his hands.

One of them hasn't been seen since—Jimmy says they got
to the hill and looked around and Jotter Deery wasn't there
anymore. In Mill Street they kicked in any doors but there
was only one house with a man in it who turned out to be
Nestor Hegarty of the old Torchmen and he was lying on the
floor in a blanket. Jimmy asked him some questions, but
Nestor was too weak—he was starved and shivering. Nestor
shook his head about knowing any Hanley. They left him
there and pulled the door back.

Jimmy took the other two with him to Hanley's sister on
Cove Lane, not far away. More of the buildings there had
people in them. They had to climb across the trench—Cove
was the first street with trenches to keep the dogs away and
anything else. Bronagh stood at the door with her new man

Roy behind her and in the back was Roy's mother with a stick.

– Yer brother's back, Jimmy told the sister.

– Is that all then? Bronagh said.

Further in they could see the shadows of ones moving about—and their voices and a man's voice started a song.

– Singing? went Jimmy.

Bronagh watched him.

– You'd need to watch yourself, Jimmy warned them, looking across the road at a destroyed house.

Bronagh laughed in his face.

– He's not shown Jimmy, Roy said.

– We have to find out what he wants, Jimmy went on. It must be something.

Bronagh spat on the ground and went back in. The old mother seemed to be sleeping up against the wall.

– You have to let us check, Roy. Inside, Jimmy said.

Charlie Nift was allowed in on his own to do the search. Charlie knew the sight of Hanley, and Jimmy thought it was less risk if he stayed on the street in case there was a trap. Jimmy and the other young one Killian Houston waited on the street—they sat in a window of a house with the roof blown out like the force had come from within the walls. All we know then is young Houston is standing in the shadows in the Ditch. None of us noticed him come back. Jimmy and Charlie turned up afterwards. Young Houston won't speak about what happened while they were waiting on the street and Jimmy laughs when you ask him. Charlie was in the Hanley house so he just shrugs—Charlie said there was about thirty of them inside the place.

Lousy Morrison was probably the next to see Hanley. There were enough reports of sightings around the town and one out on the hill near the castle and one in the sky with a balloon. Too many will say anything to make themselves big. Lousy was out on his boat and noticed a figure under the crane legs, walking around—he rowed himself in quickly and went up to the stranger. This is the way Lousy tells it.

– D'ye need a hand there son? Tell me to mind my own business like . . . but if you need a hand . . . Have you lost something?

The figure stopped but without turning around. There was just the back of him. He was in a suit and the jacket was ripped at each shoulder. Lousy sensed a bad feeling and gave room between them.

– Maybe you haven't lost something and I'm wrong. That was me out there on the boat. Did you see me?

He pointed out to where he had been in the water. The figure turned and looked at the water. There was no wind so the water was scummed and still.

– I'm sitting out there all day on the water looking for something to do. The Staff was nearly black this morning so I have to get in the boat. That's the way it goes. There's no point in arguing with it. The rats been at you there or what, with them holes? We all forget about the rats don't we? Go on. Don't be lousy. What ye after?

The one in the suit made a noise and spun round. There was the white face of a lad about twenty and the scanning famished eyes, and the lad opened his mouth and the stump of tongue flicked and poked out. The lad dropped to his knees like a dog—he was whining, Lousy swears. Lousy kicked him and ran and the lad came after him on his hands and knees. Jumping into his boat, Lousy swung the oar at him and knocked Hanley into the water. He started rowing and didn't look back and when he came marching into the Ditch, we could all tell he was annoyed and something had happened to upset his day.

157

NoNails heard it all from Lousy—Lousy didn't want to say and NoNails had to use every trick to find out. NoNails jumped up on a table. He pointed out another four of us and sent them out to the cranes. They came straight back in again, arguing among themselves about what to do when they caught sight of Hanley and whether to lay into him or what. April and some of that crowd were refusing more delay and they were gathering round the table under NoNails to have it out—they were saying that Jimmy was off the mark and had to be stopped. NoNails was thinking about it. To look at him, he was on the point of running out and doing Hanley himself just to put an end to the business. That was when Jimmy and Charlie came in the door and Jimmy walked into the middle of the crowd with the hammers in his hands. He was smiling too—a big smile on his long face and the hair tied back.

– Is young Killian in? Jimmy wanted to know.

We all looked at Jimmy.

– Aye, we heard from the corner.

Young Killian Houston was sitting on the ground, picking at the ground with his fingers, not looking up at anyone. Jimmy kept smiling but didn't say anything more to him.

– Good news, Jimmy announced to us all instead. There's things to find out.

He threw a hammer into the air and caught it by the claw on the way down.

– Like what? That was what April said to him.

– Did you get him? was shouted out.

– Lousy was lying, was shouted.

– He's a ghost. A wisp.

– We're all lying.

– It was the same before.

– The dogs dug him up.

Lousy was put up on a table and told his story again—

Lousy was annoyed and reluctant. Curtsy got up as well and showed us the handclapping. The laughing helped settle us all. Jimmy climbed up next.

– We have to catch him. In our own hands. He has to be talked to. That's what it means. There's a lot to know. All of it. That's what's going to happen. Hear that. I knew him and I owe him that. Right. Not to put him under again without a chance. The first one of yousens who touch him can look forward to me. Hear that.

April didn't like it and Jimmy landed him across the head with a hammer and he was carried outside and we left him in the road for the dogs or whatever else. April arrived in the town himself out of nowhere so he should have been more careful about shouting for blood from strangers—young Hanley wasn't exactly a stranger in any case. But we could tell Jimmy was changed for he was smiling and laughing and then he did that to April. None of April's crowd risked any more resistance. Jimmy was clear on what he wanted done next. He organised us into three groups and then we all stocked up and set out into the deadloss streets of our own place.

NoNails and us went out in a wide sweep to the fields and the sight of the castle on the hill like it had just appeared there and in again through the old cemetery. There were a few dogs around at the other end in the crypts but they cleared off and we didn't go after them. The whole town was below us in a dull mist that you couldn't see in the streets. We stayed longer than we needed among the graves—a ransacked ground, scratched up and strewn. The rats clambered through the dirt sucking on bits of bone—blowing whistle notes in the muck through the hollow shards. We looked down on the town and wondered what it must have looked like once with the river swathing through it and we all knew the sight would be the same then as now. We went on—down to the Lone Moor where the road was scraped away and sand blinded us. We crossed into Daily Crescent. Further on there was a low building without a front and we heard a noise inside it, metal sliding across bricks. We grabbed this man inside. He wasn't hiding from us. NoNails dragged him out on the road and kept him down with his foot on his back. He wasn't known. He said his name was Gibson.

– What do you want? NoNails started on him.

– Nothing. Not any more.

– Are you real?

– I am. Ask your foot.

– That's no answer. Have you seen a fella in a suit?

– Many times.

NoNails kicked him. Today. Here. I'll burn you.

– Earlier. Way over there. Up a wall.

– What was he doing?

– Dancing.

NoNails kicked him again.

– Dancing. Along the wall.

NoNails stood on his back with both feet. Nothing was said—NoNails was like a man trying to remember something. We left Gibson lying there on the ground and headed across the Ruts with that same white mass of sky over us, low and white and dented. NoNails went into the old chapel with the knife in his hand and came out and there was blood on the blade he wiped on his leg. NoNails said nothing about it and neither did we.

On along the Ruts we saw a crowd. We waited on them and it was Bronagh and her lot—about ten of them. We checked the faces for Hanley dressed up, but they were all known faces.

– Have you seen my brother? Bronagh asked.

– What's the laugh? said NoNails.

– As if you'd tell me anyway.

– Right.

– We had good times, Bronagh said.

NoNails looked away.

– He's my brother.

– We want to talk to him, said NoNails. That's what I know.

Bronagh spat at his feet. You know nothing. But listen to this—that doesn't mean you're worth believing.

NoNails walked away and we followed him through the park and up the Steep and we carried on as far as the big hall with the black brick and sat down. James started potshotting the pigeons and Shimmy climbed up the wall and got out on the roof. NoNails told James to quit the throwing and stay quiet. Then we moved inside the walls to get out of sight. Things were drawn on the walls in there—new creatures, unknown and gnarled, halfborn things and the drawings looked like lairs for them, and nests of scratches and colours and these things were out wandering the streets and would return and lapse back into the walls. James was adding a thing of his own to the gallery, chalking a marred face into the black brick. Then we heard Shimmy up above.

– Who can see what I can see?

We climbed up. Shimmy was lying flat on a narrow ledge along the rim of the wall. We all leaned out to see. Down the street there he was—Hanley walking and hopping and skipping between the ruined houses as if it was some other street he saw around him, in some other city, another time.

NoNails told us to wait until he was nearer. We watched in silence—Hanley kicking the stones in his path and sauntering in his suit through the scattered debris and stopping sometimes to look at things or put his head into the windows and he seemed to be very amused by what he saw under that white sky sinking slowly down on us. Straight below us he stopped like it was necessary. A brick dropped would have split him. He clapped his hands a few times—applauding something not there. NoNails got ready to jump down on him but James was up and away off the ledge before him and shouting and clapping his hands as he went down. Hanley stood still—like any witness he watched stunned as the man came falling out of the sky on him. James was able to get a hold of him but then he landed badly and screwed himself up on the ground and gripped his own ankle. Hanley tried to make a run for it—he kept looking back, hesitating, uncertain of what he had to do with the falling man, whether he should help. Then—when he saw NoNails hit the ground with the knife in his mouth, Hanley seemed to make up his mind and ran off. NoNails threw a brick which went near and headed after him. Shimmy followed the two of them.

We lifted James and carried him, deciding it was our best move to make a way back to the Ditch. There were four of us—Macker, Jeep Towns and James hobbling. Shimmy had taken the gun with him and there was a risk of meeting the dogs so we were moving fast. All we had was two blades that wouldn't do any damage against Grins or any of the madder mongrels. We cut down through Fairman and through the hollow buildings into the bit of scrub—the place where the well was. Jeep went up a wall and checked the road. He said there was smoke from somewhere. We took the back way down the lanes but nothing was met. We heard voices and took cover behind a levee of burnt wrecks until we saw it was Jimmy and the ones with him. Shimmy was with them as well—he said he'd lost track of NoNails and Hanley. Jimmy sent Macker and Charlie Green back to the Ditch with James. We joined up with Jimmy who was going back up the hill with some place in mind.

Jimmy was excited and—he was talking a lot and telling stories, about himself and Hanley. He had known Hanley since they were young, he was there in the fight with a crowd from the hills when Hanley died, his skull crushed under a wheel. Jimmy was saying too much, like the stories were a sudden proof that all this had to happen—Hanley reappearing, us hunting him down through the scathed city.

– He's back for a reason, Jimmy said. News.

– Bad or good?

– What if it's bad?

– The same if it's good, Jimmy laughed.

– There's worse than that, Johnstone said. There's worse than bad and good.

– Should we listen to him but?

– I know him. Right, said Jimmy. We went away together. Beyond all this. Into the hills. He wouldn't show up for nothing.

– Sure he knows where to find you if he had anything to say, Jimmy.

– I'll know when I see him. Hear that.

– Know what Jimmy?

Jimmy stopped and looked at Johnstone who had asked him what there was to know. Jimmy unhooked one of his hammers and—we all had the thought Jimmy was going to land him with it. Instead Jimmy hit the hammer against the wall of a house.

– Sold. To the fella in the nibbled suit.

In the house there was a ripping screeching sound and a layer of roof collapsed and the dust was exhaled in clouds through the windows. We all had a laugh then.

Outside a whitewashed house on Cliff Row we stopped and listened to the shouting. A few of us pushed in the door and

163

Jimmy announced who he was. Now we could hear NoNails and a woman screaming—NoNails had her against the wall under his knife and a man down on the floor wounded in the stomach. About five other ones were in the corner watching and a young one crouched at their feet like at the start of a race. Jimmy took a swipe at the wall to get calm but NoNails was still roaring into the woman's face and shouting at us at the same time that Hanley was in the place somewhere and find him. Jimmy gave NoNails a warning and hit him on the leg with the hammer.

– What do you want? NoNails said, turning on Jimmy.

– Here's a hint, said Jimmy and breathed on the knife in front of his face.

– They know, NoNails pointed the knife at the group in the corner. They know. I saw him come in. Myself. Your mucker.

Jimmy was looking at the man on the floor.

– You get them to talk, NoNails said. If they don't—they're mine. Right.

Jimmy stared back at NoNails now.

– Right? said NoNails.

Jimmy nodded but you could tell he didn't like it.

The man on the floor was Book McKeever. Jimmy had known him a long time. He took McKeever into another room and kept the rest of us out. We started searching the place with NoNails, up and down and under the floor and out in the backyard where there was a store of weapons, old weapons. We had ones surrounding the street—we were all there and other ones still turning up. When Jimmy came out of the room after a while we were silent and waited on him to speak. He stood in the middle of the room looking at the child. NoNails asked if it was his turn yet and sharpened his knife on the corner of a wall. The child—Jimmy took the child with him into the room. Not long later Jimmy came back out again and whispered to McManus who went out and took two others with him. Then from the room we heard the child scream.

– Tell me, said the mother. Please.

– Young Eamon told me what I wanted to hear, Jimmy said to her, coming near her. He touched the ends of her hair. The woman looked confused, stared at all our faces, then at the ground. We all listened to the child squealing in the other room.

– I understand, Jimmy said to the woman. Your son there knew that as well. He didn't want to. Now he's talked but. He told me. And you have to pay for talk.

– So where's the other one? said NoNails.

Jimmy kept his eyes on the woman.

– Now he's talked. You know he has to be hurt for it. It doesn't matter. Book'll do it. Book'll teach him.

– Let's get on with it, NoNails came forward. You know or not? I hope you're not letting on. For your mucker.

Jimmy moved the woman aside and got down on his knees.

– Long time, he called up the chimney. It's Jimmy. A word in your ear would make me a happy man, Misha Hanley. Come on down, Misha. There's nothing much of interest up there. I'm a keen man to talk to you Misha. Find out what you've been doing. Come on. Just think of all the things we could talk about.

There were ones on the roof started dropping stones first down the flue. Then fires were set at ground level under Hanley and flaming bits of wood dropped in from above. We could hear coughing inside the wall. Throughout it Jimmy kept talking to Hanley, calling up the chimney with memories and stories. NoNails was maddened by it—the useless talking. He went out and after a while we heard terrible agonies in the wall and the hiss of the fire going out with the boiling water. The wall was throbbing like a skin with Hanley behind it.

Jimmy must have had enough of the screaming—Jimmy started on the wall with his hammer, knocking away the bricks, and some of us joined in with our hands. We saw the feet first, blackened and no shoes. Hanley was jammed in the flue bend—the hands wedged by his side, the leg twisted and the face as red as a newborn from the boiling water. Steam was coming off him. The hair was burned away.

– Look at the state of your suit, said Jimmy to him.

The house was cleared and we all went outside and sat in the road except Jimmy and Hanley and NoNails. It was colder now and the light was tightening and lower but—we were all talking and wondering and looking forward to what would happen and any news. The child Eamon cheered up and we were all telling him about our own beatings and teachings. There was about thirty of us sitting around on the road—Indian turned up with his lot and they talked about meeting the dogs out at the Glen. Book sat upright in a doorway—he wouldn't let the wound be looked at. More ones arrived and the chimney story was told again and again. Jeep drew a picture on the ground with a nugget of tar. We all watched the front door of the house—like it was only in existence by our regard of it. One of the women started a song.

> Hitch the witch to the mast
> Tie the cry to the daydraught
> The laugh to the bolt,
> The sigh to the lock
> Take the heart
> Take the heart

Bronagh and her lot came running round the corner and stopped when they saw us all sprawled on the street in the

sunk light. Bronagh went up to the women and asked for her
brother. Some of our ones stood in front of the door to stop
her going in.

– Jimmy, she was shouting. I have a right to see my own
brother. Jimmy? I'm not going away. I've ones with me. We're
not moving.

The door was opened by NoNails.

– We're talking to him, he told her.

– And what would you have to say to him?

– Maybe nothing. Maybe too much.

Bronagh started shouting for her brother—Misha, Misha,
I'm out here.

NoNails shut the door and came over and sat down in the
street. He had the knife in his hand.

– I think I'll take a bit of air, he said. And look. It'll be dark
soon. Then what'll happen. Eh?

– Has he said anything? one of us shouted.

– It's amazing, said NoNails.

Everyone went quiet to hear. Bronagh took a step forward.

– What's he said? we all heard her ask.

– He was up the chimney, Bronagh, Lanks said. Bronagh
kept her eyes on NoNails.

NoNails started laughing—it was a hard laugh with his
own hurt in it.

– He's mine when it's done, he said then, looking at Bronagh. We've no call to be doing any of this. He should be back
where he belongs. He's not staying whatever happens. Get
used to that. Right.

Bronagh watched him and then a bad look appeared on her
face.

– To think of the nights I spent with you, she said quietly,
stepping nearer him. Do you remember them?

NoNails looked at her—a warning to be quiet.

– I don't care who is hearing, Bronagh defied him. Youse all listening? Let them listen. For I wish I could get it all wiped out, destroy us ever touching, ever seeing the sight of you, extinguish the smell of you, I'd give anything. Anything. My own skin, my brother, my eyes. You can't even imagine how much—

NoNails swiped her legs from under her with his own leg and Bronagh fell backwards on the ground. Quicker than our eyes, NoNails was above her and the knife was out. We moved as Bronagh's lot did, surrounding them.

– Imagine what? NoNails was roaring at her. Imagine what? Eh?

He looked around him—he was glaring at the road, the fractured houses, the wrecks, the trellis on the hill, the numbed sky.

– Imagine what?

He straightened up and threw the knife and it stuck firm in the centre of the door. The door opened and Jimmy was standing there and he looked at all us. He left the door tilled behind him and walked through the crowd and sat down next to Book on a step. With NoNails distracted, Bronagh rolled free and ran into the house followed by some of her ones. The rest of us waited on Jimmy.

NoNails went over to him. So tell us. What was it? Eh? What did he say then? Tell us all the big news. We're all listening to you, Jimmy. This news of yours.

Jimmy put his head in his hands.

– I know the news I have for him, NoNails said to us all. What we should have done in the first place instead of all this wanting to . . .

Jimmy turned and said something to Book McKeever beside him.

– He doesn't even know who he is, McKeever, soaked in blood, told us. He doesn't remember. Where he's been. Who

168

we are. How to talk. He's a dope. Nothing just.

We all saw Bronagh as he was talking. She came out into the road holding Hanley's hand—Hanley was scalded and battered but he was smiling craftily like a child. The two of them stood before us, solemn and beseeching and bowed. None of us had ever seen Bronagh seek mercy. We heard the dogs savaging something not far away and still no one moved or spoke. We all seemed to be waiting, like there was more to come, like we had been there before, witnessing the sister with her scalped and grinning brother back from the ground. There was a terrible stillness in the crowd—it took NoNails to shake himself free of it. He went over and grabbed Hanley by the neck. Bronagh let her brother go without a fight.

– Look. This is all it is, NoNails started saying to us, pushing Hanley around amongst us. Why the silence? Why the shame? Look. Halfboiled here. Look at him. Don't let him disgrace you. There's no shame here. Don't let there be shame. We have done nothing. He goes back where he came from. Right. And now. No more delays.

– Jimmy? Bronagh called.

– No more delays, NoNails repeated and a few of us made noises to agree.

– Jimmy? We'll just walk away. Let us just go. You knew him Jimmy.

– Don't let them shame you. Look at this thing in my hand, Jimmy shouted and lifted Hanley off the ground by the back of his neck. The lad's charred feet dangled before our eyes.

– Look at this. It's nothing. An idiot. Peeling in my hand.

A lot of us stood up in support. We were all checking how many there was on each side. It was dark now—a heavy aimless dark that seemed to leak out of us all, through our living hands and skin. Torches went on.

– Jimmy, moaned Bronagh. Don't hide. Let me have him back.

All Jimmy did was stand up and start walking up the street. He stood up in the midst of us and seemed about to speak— his eyes passed over us and then he turned and walked through us up the hill on his own and a hammer in each hand. Slowly a few more of us got up and went after him. We caught him up in the park. We went by torchlight, strung out in a line under the old trees where the birds shifted and shivered. After the park we crossed into Grafton Road. Soon in that night we forgot about NoNails and Bronagh facing each other and Hanley grinning between them—like we had been walking that way behind Jimmy for longer than any darkness or any knowledge.

We halted at the terrace. Nothing was said or wanted to be. The cold was an itch in the bones. Another trellis, about forty foot high, stood there—a hoisted grid of shrapnel. Alta says it is to give the world something to lean against and encourage it to grow again—but he is never satisfied. They are never high enough for him. We counted four fires on the hills, one of them across the water. A wind passed above our heads, salt in it and dust. Jassy was there, Donemanna Quigley, Charlie Nift, Hooks Mc Dermot, Blare, Wee Satan, Epworth Hughes, The Red, Gary Hilary of the Hilarys from the coast, Dan Feeny, Shimmer, Hax with the split ear, Henry Folds, Bleuter, Brian Riley—they were all there.

In Juniper Street Jimmy dropped the hammers and carried on. Hooks picked them up. We went through a tall building with water pouring down the walls to a lane headhigh with nettles and Jimmy passed through them like they weren't there. Donemanna offered Jimmy a torch, but he was ignored. We gathered around the bonfire spot in the field off Whitemore. Dan Feeny touched the ground and said it was hot yet.

He blew on a shard of wood and got a glow from it which cheered us.

Downwards from Beach Road was going well but—we ran into a small pack of dogs, maybe six of them. The lead was a big mongrel with a tiny head and eyes at the side like a bird. They packed in close together and their backs went up. Jimmy walked towards them with his hands by his sides. He passed through them and the animals snarled but made no go at him.

Donemanna went up the front of the line to talk to Jimmy—we all wanted to know where we were going, if anywhere. We turned the torches away from them, against the metal fences and the high steps because we were on the Crescent. A shape was lying on the steps, a man maybe, but we left it. The high fences hummed and quivered in the dark. Somebody said they were hungry and the torch beams flicked across the ground and prodded the night sky over us—spokes of light were coming out of us on all sides like we were some star fallen on a desolate planet. Then we heard Jimmy and Donemanna up ahead, climbing over a levee. We went after them but on the other side we noticed The Red was not with us anymore. Brian Riley went back up and looked for him—Riley vanished next. Blare and Epworth Hughes said they'd had enough as well and climbed back over the levee—Jimmy had lost it, they were saying, and we had to think about saving ourselves.

Jimmy led what was left of us to the Wrack Road and the grass and thorns had taken it back. We were all cut. None of us had gone out there in a long time. Jimmy went off to the side and across a field and along the old riverbed. It was colder off the roads, and muck. We went near the Pit and the smell was strong and thick like fog and the torches were weaker it seemed. We kept on the river to the fork and went with the narrow channel. The trees cover it over at points and there was a smell of the leaves in our faces—the leaves smelled new and sweet and they were hot against our faces. Hilary started a song and some of us joined in. It was better now to know we were probably aiming towards Lousy along the docks.

We could see the Staff like a tall red mast in the dark. We signalled with the torches but Lousy stayed hid until he knew who we were for sure. He came out into the fire glow with someone else—it was the Gibson one from during the day who NoNails had stood on. Gibson was in a big coat. The two of them were putting wood into the fire in the bath. The Staff was red to above our heads and then the metal was yellow on up to the tip which was invisible—a pale yellow. We were all warming our hands and leaning our faces over the flames.

– That's a good yellow, one of us said for a joke.

– There's a chance, said Lousy.

Lousy has big ideas about his staff. It's a long metal pole stuck upright in the bath. He keeps a constant fire in the bath—Lousy says the Staff is the same length a man with a knife in his back will run before he drops.

Jimmy sat away on his own. We told Lousy about Hanley but nothing was mentioned about NoNails. Lousy wanted to know what we were up to and what he could do. We all sat down on things as well, except Gibson, who kept in the fire-light. We were silent for a long time. Once we heard the dogs. Old rain blew in around us from the water and left. We were all watching the Staff for something to do—the red dulled but there was no change in the yellow. The flames died down in the bath around it—the noise of the fire died and we could all hear the bell rattling and lolling on Lousy's boat.

Soiled light swamped the docks—it was going to be the same sky again. Across the river the hills were white and unknown. Lousy and Gibson were standing close together around the fire and the Staff was hissing faintly in the morning mist. A few of us were walking round to keep warm. Jimmy was out at the edge of the docks, looking at the steaming water. Donemanna went over to him and they were talking.

– A new day, Hooks said, and clapped his hands the way Hanley did.

Jimmy walked back and stood by the fire, warming his hands.

– What do you think, Lousy?

– There was a new thing during the night. Not like what I've seen before. But I wasn't ready before maybe. A green. And smoke. Greeny smoke.

– I thought all night of going away, said Jimmy.

– To find what?

– Maybe to stop looking. They tell you it's the way there and not the arrival that matters. That's not the truth.

– No.

– No. I thought Misha might tell us something.

– He's no different than the rest of us. What can you say, Jimmy? What can you say about your life? What you've been through?

Jimmy thought for a while and then laughed.

– Where's my hammers? he said.

Hooks gave them to him. Jimmy hit the ground with one.

– Sold to the first bloody fool who wants it, he said.

We all knew we were going back then. Lousy took us back to the Ditch on the boat. He was in a great mood to have something to do.

Hanley is still around the place—he stayed on with the sister Bronagh but there's stories he's spending time with some girl now. There's no news from him. Often Jimmy goes to see him and afterwards he's silent and we all prepare for another wander around in the cold. NoNails and his crew haven't been seen. They walked off without a fight towards the far hills. Ones say they are living out there and building a place for themselves. There's others claim NoNails is in league with the dogs—he can talk to them and he's leading their attacks into our places. Ones will say anything to make themselves big. Lousy died—the Staff cooled and cracked when the fire went out after Lousy died. Gibson remains there but not much of him is seen. We sank Lousy in his boat out in the water. Jimmy will disappear for days on his own. A lot of us think he's not the same and his days are numbered. Another of us will take over—it's like Jimmy knows that and is careless and waiting.